An Amish Family Christmas

Marta Perry
and
Patricia Davids

HARLEQUIN® LOVE INSPIRED®

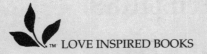

™ LOVE INSPIRED BOOKS

Recycling programs for this product may not exist in your area.

ISBN-13: 978-0-373-87920-5

An Amish Family Christmas

Copyright © 2014 by Harlequin Books S.A.

The publisher acknowledges the copyright holder of the individual works as follows:

Heart of Christmas
Copyright © 2014 by Martha Johnson

A Plain Holiday
Copyright © 2014 by Patricia MacDonald

www.Harlequin.com

Printed in U.S.A.

CONTENTS

HEART OF CHRISTMAS

Marta Perry

This story is dedicated to the wonderful editors at Love Inspired, who have taught me so much. And, as always, to Brian.

Jesus said, "I am the light of the world. Whoever follows me will never walk in darkness, but will have the light of life."
—*John* 8:12

Chapter One

Susannah Miller stood behind the security of her teacher's desk, watching the departure of school board member James Keim and his wife, and wondered if her annual Christmas program was going to spell the end of her job as teacher at Pine Creek Amish School. The hollow feeling in her stomach brought on by Keim's complaints lingered even after the door had closed behind him.

Too worldly? What would make the Keims think there was anything worldly about the Amish school's Christmas program? The program celebrated typical Amish values and attitudes toward the birth of Christ. It had always been the highlight of the school year for her scholars and their families in this small, valley community in central Pennsylvania.

Susannah stiffened her spine. It still would be, if she had anything to say about it. She glanced around the simple, one-room schoolhouse that had become so precious to her over the past twelve years. Everything from the plain, green shades on the windows to the sturdy, wooden desks to the encouraging sayings posted on the wall declared that this was an Amish school, dedicated to educating *kinder* for life in an Amish community.

Becky Shuler, Susannah's best friend since childhood,

abandoned the pretense she'd adopted of arranging books on the bookshelves. She hurried over to put her arm around Susannah's waist.

"*Ach,* Susannah, it wonders me why you don't look more upset. I'd be throwing something if I had to put up with James Keim's criticisms. The nerve of the man, coming in here and complaining about your Christmas program before he's even seen it."

Susannah shook her head, managing a smile. "I'm not upset."

Or, at least, she had no intention of showing what she was feeling. Becky was her dearest friend in the world, but she knew as well as anyone that Becky couldn't keep herself from talking, especially when she was indignant on behalf of those she loved.

"Well, you should be." Becky's round cheeks were even rosier than usual, and her brown eyes snapped with indignation. "The Keims have only lived here less than two years, and he thinks he should tell everyone else how to live Amish. How he even got on the school board is a mystery to me."

Shrugging, Susannah closed the grade book she'd been working on when the Keims had appeared at the end of the school day. "*Komm,* Becky. You know as well as I do that folks don't exactly line up to volunteer to be on the school board. James Keim was willing, even eager."

"That's certain sure." Becky's flashing eyes proclaimed that she was not going to be talked out of her temper so easily. "He was only eager to serve because he wants to make our school into a copy of the one where they lived in Ohio. All I can say is that if he liked Ohio so much, he should have stayed there instead of coming here and bothering us."

"Becky, you know you shouldn't talk that way about a brother in the faith. It's not kind."

Becky was irrepressible. "But it's true. You of all people know what a thorn in the side he's been. *Ach,* you know I wouldn't say these things to anyone but you."

"It would be best not to say them at all. James Keim has his own ideas of what an Amish school should be like. He's entitled to his opinion."

Based on his disapproving comments, Susannah suspected that Keim's previous community had been more conservative than Pine Creek, Pennsylvania. Amish churches varied from place to place, according to their membership and their bishops. Pine Creek, being a daughter church to Lancaster County, was probably a bit less stringent than what Keim had been used to.

"You're too kind, that's what you are," Becky declared, planting her fists on the edge of the desk. "You know perfectly well that he'd like to see his daughter Mary take your place as teacher, so he could boss her around all he wanted."

Susannah shook her head, but she had to admit there was some truth to what Becky said. As a thirty-year-old *maidal* who'd been teaching for a dozen years, Susannah wasn't easily cowed, at least not when it came to her classroom and the young scholars who were like her own children. Young Mary would probably be easily influenced by her father's powerful personality.

"I don't think Mary Keim has much interest in teaching, from what I've seen," she said, determined to deflect Becky's ire. Picking up the cardboard box that held Christmas program materials, Susannah set it on the desk. "If we're going to work on the program this afternoon, we'd better get started."

Becky shook her head gloomily. "Mary might not want to teach, but she'd never stand up to her *daad*. You're not going to let her help with the Christmas program, are you? She'd just be spying on you and reporting back to him."

"I'll cross that bridge when I come to it," she said. "Maybe she won't offer." Susannah pulled the tape from the box lid, sure that would divert Becky's attention.

"Just one more thing, and then I'll stop, I promise," Becky said. "You're not to pay any heed to Keim's nasty comment about you not understanding the *kinder* because you're unmarried, all right?"

"All right." That was an easy promise to make. One thing she'd never had cause to question was her feelings for her scholars.

"After all, it's not as if you couldn't have married if you'd wanted to." Becky dived into the box and pulled out a handful of paper stars. "Even after Toby left—" She stopped abruptly, her cheeks flaming. "Susannah, I'm sorry, I—"

"Forget it." Susannah forced her smile to remain, despite the jolt in her stomach at the mention of Toby's name. "I have."

That was a lie, of course, and one she should repent of, she supposed. Still, the *gut* Lord could hardly expect her to go around parading her feelings about the childhood sweetheart who had deserted her a month before their wedding was supposed to take place.

"Have you? Really?" Becky clasped her hand, her brown eyes suddenly swimming with tears.

"Of course I have," she said with all the firmness she could muster. "It was ten years ago. My disappointment has long since been forgiven and forgotten. I wish Toby well."

Did she? She tried to, of course. Forgiveness was an integral part of being Amish. But saying she forgave hadn't seemed to mend the tear in her heart.

"Well, I wish Tobias Unger was here right now so I could give him a piece of my mind," Becky declared. "He left so fast nobody had a chance to tell him how *ferhoodled* he was being. And then his getting married out in Ohio to someone he barely knew… Well, like I said, he was just plain foolish."

News of Toby had filtered back to Pine Creek after he'd left, naturally, since his family still lived here. Everyone knew he'd married someone else within a year of leaving, just as they'd heard about the births of his two children and about his wife's death last year. His mother had gone out to Ohio to help with the children for a time, and she'd returned saying that Toby and the *kinder* really ought to move back home.

But he hadn't, to Susannah's relief. She wasn't sure how she'd cope with seeing him all the time.

"Forget about him," she said. "Let's talk about how we're going to arrange the room for the Christmas program. I have some new ideas."

"You always have ideas," Becky said, apparently ready to let go of the sensitive subject. "I don't know how you keep coming up with something new every year."

"*Ach,* there's always something new to find in Christmas." Susannah felt a bubble of excitement rising in her at the thought of the much-loved season. "Maybe because we all feel like *kinder* again, ain't so?"

"I suppose so. Thomas and the twins have been whispering together for weeks now. I think they're planning a Christmas surprise for me." Becky smiled.

"Of course they are. That's what Christmas is, after all. God's greatest surprise of all for us." Susannah swung away from the desk, looking around the room. "What do you think about making the schoolroom itself surprising when folks come in? Maybe instead of having the scholars standing in the front, we could turn everything sideways. That would give the *kinder* more space."

She walked back through the rows of desks, flinging out her arms to gesture. "You see, if the audience faced this way—"

The door of the one-room school opened suddenly, interrupting her words. Susannah's heart jolted, and she felt as if she couldn't breathe.

Surely she was dreaming it. The man standing in the schoolhouse doorway wasn't...couldn't possibly be...Toby Unger.

Toby found himself standing motionless for a little too long, the words of greeting he'd prepared failing to appear. He'd known he would see Susannah, after all. He shouldn't be speechless.

William, holding on to his left hand, gave him a tug forward, while little Anna clung to his pant leg. Toby cleared his throat, feeling his face redden. He could only hope Susannah would think his flush was from the chill December air.

"Susannah. It's nice to see you after so long."

Susannah's heart-shaped face seemed to lose its frozen look when he spoke. She glanced from him to the two children, and a smile touched her lips.

"*Wilkom* to the school, Toby. These are your *kinder?*" She stooped to Anna's level. "I'm Teacher Susannah. What's your name?"

For an instant, he thought his daughter would respond, but then she hid her face against his leg, as she always did with strangers these days.

"This is Anna," he said, resting his hand on her shoulder. "She's six. And this is my son, William."

"I'm eight," William announced. "I'm in third grade."

"You're a big boy, then." Something about the expression in Susannah's green eyes made Toby wonder if she was seeing him at that age. People often said William was very like him, with his gray-blue eyes and the chestnut-colored hair that was determined to curl.

When Susannah returned her gaze to his face, there

was no longer any trace of surprise or shock in her. Her heart-shaped face had maturity and control now, although her soft peachy skin and the delicate curve of her cheek hadn't changed in the ten years since he'd seen her last.

"How nice that you could come to visit," she said. "I'm sure your *mamm* and *daad* are happy to see you and the *kinder,* especially since your father has been laid up with that broken leg from his accident."

Of course that was what she'd assume—that he was here to visit, maybe to help out after his father's fall from the barn loft. He'd made his decision so quickly there wouldn't have been time for word to spread, even though the Amish grapevine was probably still as effective as ever. Which meant he had to tell her the news that he assumed Susannah would find very unwelcome.

"We're not here to visit." He sent a quick, reassuring glance at the *kinder.* "We've come home to Pine Creek to stay."

"You're moving back?"

The question came from behind Susannah, and Toby belatedly realized there was someone else in the schoolroom. He must have been so absorbed in seeing Susannah again that he hadn't looked beyond her face. It took him a moment to recognize the woman who came quickly toward them.

"Becky Mast." He might have known that's who it would be. Becky and Susannah had been best friends since the cradle. He could just imagine how furious Becky had been at him for jilting her dearest friend all those years ago.

"I'm Becky Shuler now." She stood glaring at him, hands planted on her hips. Becky wasn't as good as Susannah at hiding her feelings, it seemed. "Are you serious about moving back to Pine Creek? Why would you?" The edge in her voice made no secret of her opinion.

"That means I'll have William and Anna in my classroom," Susannah said quickly, sending a warning look at her friend. "I'll be wonderful glad to have two new students in our school."

Becky, apparently heeding the stern glance from Susannah, seemed to swallow her ire. She smiled at the *kinder*. "Anna, are you in first grade? My twin girls are in first grade."

Anna didn't speak. He didn't expect her to. But she nodded slightly.

"The twins will enjoy having a new friend," Susannah said. "You can sit beside them, if you'd like. Their names are Grace and Mary."

"Where do the third graders sit, Teacher Susannah?" William pulled free of Toby's restraining hand. "Are there lots of boys?"

"Third graders sit right over here." She led him to a row of desks somewhere in size between the smallest ones for the beginners and the almost-adult-sized ones for the eighth graders. "We have three other boys in the third grade and four in the fourth, so you'll have lots of boys to play with at recess."

William grabbed one of the desks and lifted the top. Before Toby could correct him, Susannah had closed it again, keeping her hand on the surface for a moment.

"That is someone else's desk. We don't look through other people's things unless they say we may." Susannah's quiet firmness seemed to impress William, because he nodded and took a step back.

The confidence of her response startled him. The Susannah he remembered hadn't been capable of correcting anyone. But they were both ten years older now. They'd both grown and changed, hadn't they?

"I hope it's not a problem to add two new scholars into your classroom in the middle of the year," he said.

His mind wandered to the things he'd have to tell Susannah about the *kinder,* sooner or later. Things that had made him return home, seeking help and stability from his parents.

There was William's talent for mischief making. And Anna's shyness, which seemed to be getting worse, not better. But something in him balked at the thought of confessing his failings as a parent to Susannah, of all people.

With her hand resting on the nearest desk, Susannah seemed very much at ease and in command in her classroom. "Becky, would you mind taking William and Anna out to join the twins on the swings? I have some papers their *daadi* must fill out."

Becky nodded and held out her hands to the children. "*Komm.* I'll show you the playground."

To his surprise, Anna took Becky's hand and trotted alongside her with only one backward glance. William, of course, raced ahead of them. After a pause at the door to allow Becky to grab a jacket against the winter chill, they went outside.

"*Denke,* Susannah." He turned back to her. "I wanted a chance to talk without the children overhearing."

"Of course." Her tone was suddenly cool and formal. She walked to the teacher's desk and retrieved a folder from a drawer, not speaking. Then she turned back to him. "Here are some forms you can fill out and return when you bring the *kinder* to class. Will you want them to start tomorrow?"

He nodded as he took the papers, hesitating in the face of her frosty demeanor. It was as if all Susannah's gentle friendliness had left the room with his *kinder.*

Still, he could hardly expect her to welcome him back, not after what he'd done. Groping for something to say, he noticed the Christmas stars strewn across her desk, and the sight made him smile.

"Is it time for the Christmas program already? Some things never change, ain't so?"

Susannah nodded, her expression brightening. "It wouldn't seem like Christmas if we didn't have the school Christmas program to look forward to. Becky and I were just saying that the challenge is to come up with something new every year."

"It's not possible, is it?" He felt a sudden longing to keep her smiling, to keep her from thinking about their past. "Except that someone usually makes a new and different mistake each time."

Susannah leaned against the desk, her face relaxing just a little. "I seem to remember a few mistakes that might have been intentional. Like a certain boy who mixed up the letters in the word the class was supposed to be spelling out, so that our Merry Christmas greeting didn't make any sense."

He grinned at the memory. "Don't mention that to William, or he'll try to outdo my mischief making."

"I'll keep your secret," she said, the corners of her lips curving, making the words sound almost like a promise.

For a moment they stood looking at each other, and he felt as if they were sixteen years old again, knowing each other so well they hardly needed words to communicate. How was it that the past ten years had disappeared so quickly and the link between them still remained?

"Susannah, I hope—" He stopped, not sure he wanted to go on with what he'd impulsively begun.

"What?" Her eyebrows lifted, her green eyes open and questioning, just like they used to be before he'd given her cause to regard him with wariness and suspicion.

He sucked in a breath, determined to get the words out before he lost his courage. "I just hope my return isn't… well, difficult for you…after the way we parted."

After the way he'd panicked as their wedding date grew

closer, bolting in the night with only a short note left behind to explain himself.

All the vitality seemed to leave Susannah's face. She turned, taking a step away from him. The moment shattered as if it had never happened.

"Of course not." Susannah's voice was colorless, her voice that of a stranger. "I'm sure everyone in Pine Creek will be happy to *wilkom* you home."

Toby carefully smoothed the papers he'd clenched in his hand. Susannah didn't need words to spell out what she felt. It was only too clear.

She hadn't forgotten, and she hadn't forgiven.

Chapter Two

Susannah held her breath, fearing her denial hadn't been very convincing. If she wasn't bothered by Toby's return to Pine Creek, why did she find it necessary to hide her expression from him?

Because he'd always been able to read her emotions too clearly, answered a small voice in her thoughts. Because she was afraid that the feelings between them might still be there.

Grow up, she told herself fiercely and swung around to face him. She touched her desk with the tips of her fingers, and the reminder of who and where she was seemed to steady her.

"It's been a long time." She hoped her smile was more natural now. "I'm sure people will chatter about us, remembering that we planned to marry. But if we show them that we are nothing more than old friends, that should silence the gossip, ain't so?"

If he believed her only concern was what people might say, so much the better. And it was certain sure the grapevine would wag with this tale for a time.

"If you can stand it, I can." Toby's smile was full of relief. It relaxed the tight lines of his face, making him look more like the boy she remembered.

As for the rest... Well, Toby had changed, of course. Maybe men changed more between twenty and thirty than women did. Toby seemed taller, broader, even more substantial in a way. He looked as if it would take a lot to move him.

His hair, always the glossy brown of horse chestnuts, might be a shade darker, but she'd guess it still had glints of bronze in the sun. His eyes were a deep, deep blue, but there were tiny lines at the corners of them now, no doubt because of the difficult time he'd been through with his wife's death. His curly dark beard hid his chin, but she had no doubt it was as stubborn as ever.

Realizing she was studying his face too long, Susannah said, "Tell me a little about your young ones. Have they had a difficult time adjusting to their *mammi*'s death?"

Toby nodded. He perched on one of the first grader's desks, looking like a giant amid the child-size furniture. "It hasn't been easy. It's been over a year, you know. I suppose I thought her loss would become less hurtful for them after a time, but that doesn't seem to be happening."

"I'm sorry." Her heart ached at his obvious pain. Poor children. Poor Toby, trying to deal with them and cope with his own grief, as well. "There isn't any timetable for grief, I'm afraid. For a child to lose his or her mother is devastating."

"It is." He rubbed the back of his neck in a gesture so familiar that it made her heart lurch. "I feel like a pretty poor substitute for Emma in their eyes."

"They need you to be their father, not their mother," she said gently. "Was your wife's family not able to help?"

Toby hunched his shoulders. "They had moved to Colorado to help start a new settlement before Emma became sick. Her mother came for a time, but I can't say it helped a lot. She was so sad herself that it seemed to make the pain even worse for the *kinder*."

"So that's why you decided to come back home." It was growing easier to talk to him with every word. Soon it wouldn't bother her at all, and she could treat Toby just as she would any other friend of her childhood.

"That's so. I knew I needed more help, and my folks kept urging me to come. Then *Daad*'s accident seemed to make it more crucial." Toby shifted a little, maybe finding the small desk not well suited for sitting on. His black jacket swung open, showing the dark blue shirt he wore, which nearly matched his eyes. "*Daad* has always wanted me to work with him in the carriage-building business." He abruptly stopped speaking, leaving Susannah to think there was more to his decision than he'd admitted.

"Is that what you want, too?"

Toby's face lit up. "More than anything. Working with *Daad* was always the future I'd planned for myself, before I…left."

Susannah had been so wrapped up in her own loss ten years ago that she'd never thought about what Toby had given up when he'd run away from their impending wedding.

"Well, it's *gut* that you can join him now." She forced a cheerful note into her voice. "Especially since he's laid up. Although I don't suppose he's as busy in the winter, anyway, is he?"

"No. *Daad* says if he had to fall out of the hayloft, he picked the best time to do it. He'd intended to keep working over the winter, but all he's been able to do is supervise some repairs with Ben doing the work. And constantly criticizing, according to Ben." He chuckled.

Ben, Toby's younger brother, had been one of Susannah's scholars only a few years ago.

Susannah hesitated, but there was a question she wanted answered, and since they were talking so freely, maybe it was best just to get it out.

"I hope you didn't delay your return all this time because of what happened between us." That was as close as she could come to asking him outright.

Toby's eyes widened. "No, Susannah. Please don't think so. The truth is that Emma didn't want to move away from her family and the community she'd always known." He shrugged. "I didn't much like working in a factory, but I couldn't bear to tear her away from her family."

No, she could imagine that Toby hadn't been well suited to factory work. He'd always wanted to do things his own way and at his own pace. "You made the best decisions you could, I'm sure."

Toby's face tightened, and she had a sense of things unsaid. "Well, I'm here now, anyway. I thought Ben might resent me joining the business, but he seems wonderful glad to have someone else for *Daad* to blame when things go wrong." His face relaxed in a grin. "*Daad*'s a little testy since he can't do things on his own."

"I'm sure. Your *mamm* mentioned that she had her hands full with him."

"That she does. I'm afraid it's an added burden, me returning with the two *kinder*. But I didn't know what else to do."

"*Ach,* don't think that way." She nearly reached out to him in sympathy but drew back just in time. She couldn't let herself get too close to Toby, for both their sakes. "You know your parents want nothing more than to have you and their grandchildren with them. Your *mamm* is always talking about the two of them."

"She may not be so happy when she realizes what she's got herself into." He stared down at his hands, knotted into fists against his black broadfall trousers. "The truth is, William and Anna are both…difficult."

Susannah had the sense that this was what Toby had been trying to say since the *kinder* had left the room, and she murmured a silent prayer for the right words.

"Difficult how?" She tried to smile reassuringly. "You don't need to be afraid to confide in me, Toby. Anything you tell me about the *kinder* is private, and as their teacher, I can help them best if I understand what's happening with them."

He nodded, exhaling a long breath. "I know I can trust you, Susannah." A fleeting smile crossed his face, then was gone. "I always could."

No doubt he was remembering all the times she hadn't told on him when he'd been up to mischief. "Just tell me what troubles you about them," she said.

"My little Anna," he began. "Well, you saw how she is. So shy she hardly ever says a word. She was never as outgoing as William, but she used to chirp along like a little bird when it was just the family. Now she scarcely talks even to me."

Susannah's heart twisted at his obvious pain. "Is it just since her *mammi* died?"

He nodded. "That's when I started noticing it, anyway. She hasn't even warmed up to her *grossmammi* yet, and I know that hurts my mother."

"She'll be patient," Susannah said, knowing Sara Unger

would do anything for her grandchildren. "What about William? He's not suffering from shyness, I'd say."

"No." Toby didn't smile at her comment. If anything, he looked even more worried. "William has been a problem in another way." He hesitated, making her realize how difficult it was for him to talk about his children to her. "William has been getting up to mischief."

"Well, he probably takes after his father. You shouldn't—"

He shook his head, stopping her. "I'm not talking about the kind of pranks I used to play. I'm talking about serious things. Things where he could have been badly hurt." He paled. "He tried to ride bareback on a young colt that was hardly broken to harness. He challenged one of the other boys to jump from the barn window, and it's a wonder he wasn't hurt." Toby's jaw tightened. "He started a fire in the shed. If I hadn't seen the smoke—" He broke off abruptly.

Susannah's thoughts were reeling, but she knew she had to reassure him somehow. Say something that would show she was on his side.

"I'm so sorry, Toby." Her heart was in the words. "But you mustn't despair. William is young, and he's acting out his pain over his mother in the only way he can think of. This is going to get better."

"I want to believe that." The bleakness in his expression told her he didn't quite mean what he said.

"There's a way to reach William, I promise you. I'll do everything I can to help him. To help both of them."

Wanting only to ease the pain she read in Toby's face, she reached out to clasp his hand. The instant they touched, she knew she'd made a mistake.

Their eyes met with a sudden, startled awareness. His seemed to darken, and Susannah felt her breath catch in her throat. For a long moment, they were motionless, hands clasped, gazes intertwined.

And then he let go of her hand as abruptly as if he'd touched a hot stove. He cleared his throat. "*Denke,* Susannah." His voice had roughened. "I knew the *kinder* could count on you for help."

She clasped her hands together tightly, feeling as if she'd forgotten how to breathe. "That's why I'm here," she said. She managed a bland smile and retreated behind her desk.

Toby rose, and for the life of her, she couldn't think of anything else to say. But one thing had become very clear to her.

She wasn't over Toby Unger at all, and somehow, she was going to have to learn to deal with it.

Toby sat at the kitchen table by lamplight with *Daad* while *Mamm* put dishes away. He felt as if he'd jumped backward in time. He and *Daad* used to sit like this in the evening when the chores were done, hearing the life of the household go on around them while *Daad* planned out their next day's work.

The two sisters who'd come after him were married now, with families of their own, but his youngest sister, Sally, was upstairs putting William and Anna to bed for him. Sixteen, and just starting her *rumspringa* years, Sally had developed into a beauty, but she didn't seem aware of it. Maybe she thought it was natural to have all the boys flocking around her the way they did. It didn't turn her head, at any rate. She was sweet and loving with his children—an unexpected blessing upon his return.

And Susannah? Would she be a blessing, as well? He still felt that jolt of surprise he'd experienced when their eyes first met. How could he still feel an attraction for the woman he'd jilted ten years ago?

Mamm leaned across him to pour a little more coffee into *Daad*'s cup. "Did you have a chance to talk to Susannah today about the *kinder?*"

He nodded. He had to keep his mind on his children. Any flicker of attraction he felt for Susannah was surely just a result of seeing someone again he'd once been so close to.

"It wasn't easy to tell her," he admitted. "But I figured she needed to know about my worries if she's going to be their teacher."

"You don't need to worry about Susannah. She's not one to go blabbing about private things." *Daad*'s voice was a low bass rumble. He shifted position on the chair, and Toby suspected the heavy cast on his leg was troubling him.

"She's a fine teacher," *Mamm* said warmly. "Look how patient she was with that boy of Harley Esch's when he had trouble learning. And now he's reading just as well as can be, his *mamm* told me. She can't say enough about Teacher Susannah."

"I'm glad to know it. I hope she does as well with William and Anna." Toby raised his gaze to the ceiling, hoping that William wasn't upstairs giving his young aunt any trouble.

"*Ach,* you're worrying too much." His mother patted his shoulder, fondly letting her hand rest there. "You'll see. Just being here with family is going to do them a world of good. And Susannah will help them, too."

Toby nodded, smiling, and wished he could share her confidence. The thing he couldn't talk about, never even thought about if he could help it, reared its ugly head.

If he hadn't rushed into marriage with Emma, if he had

been a better husband, if he had been able to love her as much as he should have...

Once started, that train of thought could go on and on. He had to stop before the burden of guilt grew too heavy to carry.

"We've been fortunate to have Susannah settle in and teach for over ten years," *Mamm* said. "It's not often that a teacher stays so long. Usually just when they have experience, they up and get married—" She stopped abruptly, maybe thinking she was getting into rocky territory.

Was he the reason Susannah had never married? If so, he'd done even more harm than he'd known.

"I hear James Keim is saying she's been there too long," *Daad* commented, stretching his good leg.

Toby frowned. "Who is James Keim, and why would he be saying something like that?"

"*Ach,* I'm sure he means no harm," *Mamm* said quickly. "He and his family moved here from Ohio a couple of years ago, and he's certain sure interested in the school. He was even willing to serve on the school board."

That didn't really answer his question. "Why would he say something negative about Susannah?"

"Well, now, we don't know for sure that he did," *Daad* said in his calm way. He sent a quelling glance toward *Mamm.* "It was gossip, when all's said and done. But supposedly he thinks the school would be better off with a new, young teacher, someone closer to the students in age."

"That's nonsense." Toby's tone was so sharp that both his parents looked at him. He shrugged. "I mean, it seems silly to think of getting rid of a good teacher for a reason like that. Like *Mamm* said, the more experience a teacher has, the better."

Toby wondered to himself, where had that come from, that protective surge of feeling for Susannah? And more important, what was he going to do about it?

Chapter Three

When Susannah took her scholars outside for recess, she had a moment to assess William and Anna's first day of school. It would be hard to forget, since Anna was still clinging firmly to her skirt.

Normally, Susannah might opt to stay inside during recess and prepare for the next class, but her helper today was Mary Keim, and she suspected Mary wasn't ready to be left alone with the *kinder* yet. She studied the girl's face for a moment, searching for some sign that Mary actually wanted to be helping at the school. She couldn't find one. Mary stood pressed against the stair railing, not venturing toward the swings and seesaws, which occupied most of the children. She seemed afraid to move.

Susannah bit back a wave of exasperation. She rather expected this withdrawal from shy little Anna on her first day at a new school. She would think that sixteen-year-old Mary might have a bit more confidence.

"You don't need to stay here with me, Mary. Why don't you play catch with the older children? Or you can push some of the young ones on the swings."

Mary showed the whites of her eyes like a frightened horse. "I...I'll try," she said and walked slowly toward the swings.

No, not a horse, Susannah decided, watching the girl's tentative approach to the smaller children. Mary was more like a little gray mouse, with her pale face, pointed chin and anxious, wary eyes. She feared making a mistake, Susannah decided, and so she took refuge in doing nothing. If her father thought a few weeks as the teacher's assistant was going to turn the girl into a teacher, he was mistaken.

Well, parents were often the last to realize what their children were best suited for. She'd certainly seen that often enough as a teacher. But she had more immediate problems to deal with than Mary Keim's future.

Sinking onto the step, Susannah drew Anna down next to her. "You did very well with your reading this morning, Anna. Do you like to read?"

The child nodded, her blue eyes showing a flicker of interest, but she didn't speak.

"I'd guess somebody reads stories to you before you go to bed at night. Am I right?"

Again a nod, this time accompanied by a slight smile.

"Let's see if I can guess who. Is it *Daadi?*"

A shake of the head answered her.

"Grossmammi?"

"Sometimes." The word came in a tiny whisper.

"Who else, besides *Grossmammi?*" Why wasn't Toby doing it? Was he that busy with the carriage business at this time of the year? Maybe he considered that a woman's job, but...

"Aunt Sally likes to read stories."

That was the longest sentence she'd gotten from the child, and Susannah rejoiced.

"I know your aunt Sally. Once she was one of my scholars, just as you are. She liked to read then, too."

Anna's small face lit up. "She makes all the noises in the story when she reads."

Susannah couldn't help chuckling. "She did that in school, too. Do you giggle when she does it?"

And there it was—an actual smile as Anna nodded. Susannah put her arm around the child and hugged her close. All Anna needed was a little time, patience and encouragement. She would—

A sudden shout jolted Susannah out of her thoughts. She turned her head, her gaze scanning the schoolyard for trouble. And found it. Two boys were engaged in a pushing match, and even as she ran toward them, she realized that the smaller one was William.

"Stoppe, schnell," she commanded in the tone that never failed to corral her students' attention. It didn't fail now. Both William and Seth Stoltzfus, a sixth grader with a quick temper, jerked around to face her.

"This is not acceptable. Into the schoolroom. Now. Both of you." With a hand on each one's shoulder, she marched them toward the school.

Mary stood watching, openmouthed.

"Mary, you are in charge on the playground until I ring the bell. Try to get Anna to go on the swings with the twins, please."

Mary nodded and scurried to do her bidding, and Susannah sent up a quick prayer for guidance. After what Toby had confided to her, she'd expected trouble with William, but she hadn't thought it would flare up so quickly.

"Now then." Leaving them standing in front of her desk, she took her place behind it. "What did you think you were doing?"

"He started it," Seth said quickly.

"Did not," William retorted. "He did."

"Did n—"

"Stop." She halted the repetition of blame. "Were you arguing over the baseball?" Some of the older boys had been tossing it around before the trouble started.

Seth nodded. "It went toward him, and he wouldn't give it back."

"I *was* going to throw it." William glared belligerently. "You didn't need to grab."

"So, you were both wrong," she said. "That is not how we settle disputes in our school. You know that. You'll both stay after school and wash the boards for me today." She knew that would make an impact. While the girls vied for the opportunity to clean the chalkboards, the boys hated the job. For some reason she didn't understand, they'd decided it was unmanly.

"*Yah,* Teacher Susannah." Seth edged backward, and when she didn't say anything more, he hurried back to his interrupted recess.

William took a few steps, his expression hostile, then stopped. "Are you going to tell my *daadi?*"

Susannah's heart softened. "I don't think that's necessary."

The expression that swept across his face couldn't be missed. Disappointment. Why was the boy disappointed? Relief would be more natural, wouldn't it?

Jaw set, William turned away, contriving to knock the books off the nearest desk as he did so.

"Perhaps I *should* ask your father to come in," she said, watching for his reaction.

William shrugged. "He can't. He's busy working all the time."

Susannah surveyed the boy thoughtfully. That surely wasn't true, but she had a feeling William thought it was. Possibly this attitude was a hangover from what must have been very difficult times. Toby had been working in a factory, he'd said, so he wouldn't have been able to take time off during the day very often.

Most Amish, if they could manage it, preferred to farm or run a home-based business so that the family could work together. Toby apparently hadn't had that choice, and with a sick wife and no relatives close at hand, he'd probably had little time for anything else.

"It might be different here," she suggested, concerned that she might be venturing too far into personal territory.

William shook his head, pressing his lips together. "Can I go?"

She nodded, feeling helpless, and watched him leave the room with a swagger probably designed to tell anyone who saw him that he didn't care about getting into trouble with the teacher.

She really didn't want to have any further private conversations with Toby, but she was afraid she'd have to.

The opportunity arose when Toby came to pick up his children from school. After a look at his son, busily washing the chalkboards, he walked out of the schoolhouse and approached Susannah where she stood on the steps, waving goodbye to her scholars.

"I take it William is in trouble already." He stood at the top of the steps, looking down at her.

Susannah went up a step. Toby had quite enough of a height advantage on her already, without adding any more. "I'm afraid so."

He looked as if he was bracing himself for the news. "How bad?"

"Not bad at all." She smiled to lessen the sting he was undoubtedly feeling. No parent wanted to hear that his child hadn't behaved properly. "I thought a session of washing the boards together might be good for both Seth and William."

Toby put one hand on the porch post, looking as if he'd like to pull it loose and throw it. "Fighting?"

"Just pushing each other. There's no need for you to say anything more to him. I can deal with what happens at my school."

"I'm sure you can." His glance held a hint of surprise. "You've changed, Susannah."

"I've grown up," she corrected. "We both have."

He blew out a sigh. "I don't know. Grown-ups are supposed to have the answers, aren't they? I don't seem to have any."

"No one does. We just muddle along and do our best to live as God wants."

She'd had every intention of keeping her conversations with him cool and impersonal, and here they were, talking like old friends again. Like people who'd known each other so long that they barely needed to use words.

"What can I do, Susannah?" He was looking at her, his eyes so honest and pleading that she knew she had to help him, no matter the risk to her heart.

"I've been giving it some thought," she said carefully. "It seems to me that Anna just needs a bit of time and patience to ease her transition to her new life. As for William..." She had to proceed slowly. She didn't want to add to Toby's burdens, but he seemed to be the key to the boy's difficulties. "Perhaps if you could spend more time with him—"

"Do you think I don't know that I'm to blame?" The quick flash of anger seemed to be directed more at himself than at her. "That's the main reason I moved back here. I want William to have the kind of relationship with me that I had with my *daad,* working together, enjoying each other...." His voice trailed off.

"I know," she said softly. "I thought perhaps if you volunteered to help with the Christmas program, it would be a start. William could work with you building the props and getting the classroom ready. And Anna would find reassurance in having you close at hand during part of her school day."

And what would she find in having Toby in her classroom, seeing him often, trying to manage her rebellious heart?

But Toby's face had already brightened at her suggestion. "That's a fine idea, Susannah. If you're sure you can stand having me around so much, that is."

She couldn't force a smile no matter how hard she tried, but she nodded. "*Gut.* That's settled, then. We'll start work on the program on Monday afternoon."

"I'll be here," he said. He started to turn toward the classroom and his *kinder,* and then stopped, looking into her face. "You're a kind person, Susannah. I won't forget this."

His fingers brushed her hand, and awareness shimmered across her skin. No. She wouldn't forget, either.

Susannah sat beside Becky in the buggy on Saturday, struggling to find the best way of telling her friend she was going to be working with Toby. There didn't seem to be any.

Becky was bound to disapprove, and Susannah could hardly blame her. After all, it was Becky who'd seen her through that terrible time after Toby left.

Back then, Susannah had managed to keep her calm facade in place with other people. That had been prideful, most likely, but it had seemed necessary. She hadn't wanted to burden her parents or Toby's with her hurt. It was only with Becky that she'd felt free to expose her inner grief and pain.

They were pulling into the parking area at Byler's Book Shop, and she still hadn't managed to bring up the subject. Byler's, like most Amish businesses, was located right on the family farm—a square, cement-block building to house the store, run by Etta Byler, with the help of various sisters and cousins.

Becky parked the buggy at the hitching rail, and they

both slid down. "I love having a reason to visit the book shop." Becky was smiling in anticipation. "I think I'll get a book for each of the twins for Christmas. After I help find the materials for the program, of course."

"You can do all the browsing you want," Susannah said, leading the way to the door. "That's the best part of coming to the book shop, ain't so?"

Susannah paused inside the door, taking in the sections devoted to children's books, history and the ever-popular Amish romance novels. Several women were already browsing through books by their favorite authors. Becky cast a longing look in that direction, but she followed Susannah to the area devoted to aids for teachers.

Susannah paused in front of a display of bulletin-board materials. "I was thinking that we might work the whole program around the idea of light. Jesus came to be the light for the world, and then there's the Christmas star and the idea of letting your light shine...."

"But not blinding your neighbor with it," Becky finished the familiar Amish phrase, grinning. "That's a great idea, if we can find enough things that relate to it."

"I can write some of the pieces myself, if I need to." The youngest scholars were usually the most difficult to find parts for. They needed roles that didn't require too much reading and would allow them to move around, if possible. They'd be fidgeting, anyway, unused to being the center of attention for all the parents and grandparents and siblings who would pack the schoolhouse for the event.

"Stars, candles," Becky said, musing. "Or even lanterns. We have some in the barn."

"I've been thinking of having two or three large cardboard candles on each side of the area where the scholars will perform. They'd enjoy that, I think."

Becky nodded, quick to jump on the idea. "We can get

some of the fathers to make them, ain't so? Who do you want to ask?"

Susannah couldn't put it off any longer. At least no one was close enough to hear Becky's inevitable reaction.

"I already have a volunteer." She kept her voice casual and her eyes on the shiny cutouts she was leafing through. "Toby is willing to help."

It took so long for Becky to respond that Susannah thought she hadn't heard. She grabbed Susannah's hands and pulled her around to face her.

"Toby? What is wrong with you, Susannah? Why would you let Toby anywhere near you after what he's done?"

"Shh. Becky, his children are my students. I can't keep him away from the school." She had no hope that Becky would accept that as a reason.

"I know what he's doing." Becky's eyes narrowed. "He's volunteered to help because he wants to get close to you again."

Her voice had risen, and Susannah shot a quick look around. "Hush. Do you want someone to hear?" At least in a public place, she had a reason for trying to mute Becky's protests. Unfortunately she knew she'd have to listen to them all the way home.

Becky dismissed her words with a quick gesture. "Why didn't you tell him no? Say you already had enough help?"

"It wasn't that way." She found she was trying to avoid her friend's eyes. "Toby didn't suggest it. I did."

Becky was silent for a moment, clasping her hands tightly. "*Ach,* Susannah, what were you thinking? You're surely not falling for him again."

"It's nothing like that," she protested. "William is troubled, and he needs attention from his father. I thought if they worked together on the project, it might help him."

Becky pressed her lips together in disapproval. "Let him do that outside of school—far away from you."

"You don't have to worry about me. My only interest in Toby is as his children's teacher. I'm not going to get involved with him again."

Becky studied Susannah's face for a moment and shook her head. "I'm not sure if you actually believe what you're saying or not. But I am sure of one thing. If you let Toby get close to you, he'll only hurt you again."

Susannah felt her throat tighten as she considered the words. Becky was only saying what she herself knew was true. But her commitment to her students came before her own feelings. Somehow, she'd have to get through working with Toby without exposing her heart.

Chapter Four

Toby felt more than a little out of place when he arrived at the school Monday afternoon for his first stint helping with the Christmas program. Susannah had seemed confident that this would be good for his children, but he couldn't deny it made him self-conscious to think of trying to build bridges with his children under her gaze.

Well, Susannah wouldn't be critical of him. That wasn't in her nature. He'd turned his *kinder* over to her with complete confidence in her abilities, so the least he could do was follow her advice.

The schoolroom was already humming with activity when he stepped inside, and Toby paused for a moment, hefting his toolbox in one hand, while he tried to make sense of what was going on. One group of children seemed to be reading their parts out loud, while in another corner, some older girls were working on poster-size sheets of paper.

Becky was there, directing a group that was decorating a bulletin board. She gave him a cool nod, making him wonder what she'd said when she'd learned he'd be helping. Nothing complimentary, he imagined.

Susannah greeted him, wearing her usual composed smile. "You're right on time. I have the materials over here for the big candles, and I thought you and some of the boys might start on those first."

He nodded, following her to one side of the room where some desks had been pushed out of the way. She'd described what she wanted, and it seemed simple enough, although time-consuming, especially since Susannah expected him to be working with the children instead of doing it himself. Still, that was a typically Amish way of learning—doing a task alongside someone who had already mastered it.

Almost before he had gathered his thoughts, Susannah left him alone with a group of boys that included his son. William wore a wooden expression that suggested he wasn't sure if he liked having his father here in the schoolroom.

"Suppose you all gather 'round, and I'll show you what Teacher Susannah wants us to build." He spread out the drawing he'd made for them. "The candles will be supported by a base and a diagonal, wooden brace on the back, where it won't show." He pointed with his pencil, and several of the older boys nodded.

"We'll be painting them when they're finished, ain't so?" One of them, a tall kid with a shock of wheat-colored hair brushing his eyebrows, asked as he leaned over the sketch.

Toby nodded. "We've got a lot of work to do before then, so let's get started."

To his relief, several of the older boys immediately caught on to what was required. They had obviously done some carpentry before. He was able to set them to work on one candle while he tackled another with the younger ones, and soon the tap of hammers joined in the chorus of children's voices practicing their lines under Susannah's direction.

"You started school here at the right time," he told William. "Putting on the Christmas program is one of most fun things you'll ever do in the Pine Creek school, ain't so?"

His son shrugged. "I guess."

Toby inwardly sighed. If he got discouraged every time William gave him a two-word answer, he'd be done before he started. He had to persevere.

"My *daadi* says you went to school here with him." The boy working next to William had a face spattered with freckles and a gap-toothed smile.

Memory stirred. "Is your *daadi* Paul Broder?"

The kid's grin widened as he nodded. "I'm Matthew Broder. Do you remember my *daad*?"

"I sure do. Ask him if he remembers the time we ate the green apples from the apple tree in the schoolyard and were sick all afternoon."

The memory brought a smile to his face. Paul had often been his partner in crime, as he recalled, but he hadn't trusted Toby's judgment quite so much after the green-apple affair.

William made a pretense of ignoring them, but he suspected his son was more interested in the conversation than he let on.

"Teacher Susannah was in school here with us, too," he said. "Did your *daad* tell you that?"

Matthew nodded. "Everybody knows that."

Of course. Everybody knew everything there was to know about people in this isolated community. Funny how he'd once been so eager to leave, when now he just wanted to fit in again.

Holding a crosspiece for the base while his son hammered a nail in, Toby realized he hadn't felt this content in a long time. It was good to be back in the familiar schoolroom, feeling again the sense of order and purpose that permeated it.

And it was especially satisfying to be working next to his son, watching William's small hands mimic his actions. This was what they could have had all along, if he hadn't been stuck working in the factory all day and getting home so late that he hardly saw his *kinder*.

But he'd known what to expect when he got married. Emma hadn't made any secret of her feelings. He just hadn't expected their marriage to turn out the way it had.

By the time Susannah rang the bell signaling the end of the school day, they'd made good progress on the first two candles. He glanced over to catch Susannah's eye.

"I'll stick around for a few more minutes to finish up, if that's okay."

She nodded, supervising as her scholars lined up to leave, obviously preoccupied with seeing that they had coats, jackets, books, lunch pails and so forth. In a moment the schoolroom had emptied, but Becky lingered, her jacket in her hands and the twins tugging at her skirt.

"I told my mother we'd pick her up right after school," she was telling Susannah, sounding unduly concerned about something so simple.

"Of course. Go ahead." Susannah picked up a pencil that had dropped on the floor.

"Are you sure?" Becky paused with a meaningful glance at him.

"Go." Susannah made a shooing motion with her hands.

Despite her doubts, Becky went out the door with her twins.

Once the door had closed behind them, Toby grinned at Susannah. "Is Becky worried about my reputation or yours?"

A faint color came up in Susannah's cheeks. "I...neither, I'm sure."

Her reaction took him aback. Maybe this was more than just a matter of Becky disliking him for jilting Susannah.

He thought of what *Daad* had said about the school board member. Was Susannah's position really so precarious that she couldn't be in the schoolroom with a man she'd known all her life? Or was Becky afraid Susannah still had feelings for him? Either way, he'd best be careful.

Anna tugged at Susannah's apron. "Teacher? Were you really in school with my *daadi?*"

Apparently Anna's curiosity had overcome her shyness. He was so relieved he rushed to answer. "She was. And so was the twins' mother."

Anna blinked, absorbing this news.

"Your *daadi* grew up here in Pine Creek," Susannah explained. "So this was his school. When we were in first grade, like you, I sat here." She led Anna to the desk she'd occupied in the first row. "And he sat right across from me, where you sit now."

"Really?" Anna seemed to look at her desk with fresh eyes. "Did you really sit here, *Daadi?*"

"Teacher Susannah is right as usual," he said solemnly. "In fact, if no one has sanded it out, my initial might still be under the seat." Crossing to them, he turned the seat over and showed her. "See?"

Susannah looked at him with amusement in her eyes. She bent to run her fingers over the letters he'd dug with the point of a compass, bringing her face close to his. "I can see I'll have to have these refinished."

Her nearness brought a treacherous memory to mind. He'd taken Susannah home from a singing for the first time—*Daad* had let him take the two-seater buggy. He'd been so determined—and so nervous—to kiss her, it was a wonder he'd ever got up the courage.

He'd stopped the buggy just beyond the glow from her parents' kitchen window. Turned to her, just able to make out the soft curve of her lips. She'd smiled at him and then, maybe reading his intent in his face, her smile had trembled. Their lips had met—an awkward kiss that carried with it all the sweetness of first love.

Maybe the memory showed in his face too clearly. Susannah's eyes met his, and they darkened. Her lips trembled, and for a moment, he was transported back to that buggy on a spring night....

The schoolroom door clattered open, and heavy footsteps sounded. Fear flared in Susannah's eyes.

Moving deliberately, he righted the desk, setting it squarely upright. Then he turned to meet James Keim's unfriendly scrutiny.

"James Keim, isn't that right? I'm Tobias Unger."

"I know who you are." Keim glanced from Susannah to him. "What are you doing here?"

The question was almost openly hostile.

Anger flared, but before he could speak, Susannah did.

"Toby has two *kinder* in our school." Her tone was perfectly cool, and Toby wondered what it took to keep it that way.

Keim's face settled into a disapproving frown. "It's after school hours."

Toby clenched the edge of the desk hard enough to turn his knuckles white. Susannah flashed him a look that spoke volumes.

"We are working on preparations for the Christmas program." Susannah gestured toward the half-finished candles. "Toby generously volunteered to work with the boys on some carpentry. We always need parents to help." She looked at Keim expectantly, and Toby had to suppress a smile. Obviously the man didn't want to help. Just as obviously he didn't want to admit it.

Keim cleared his throat. "You know how I feel about this program of yours. But I'll have Mary come help you. It will be more suitable than having the teacher alone in the schoolroom with a man."

Clutching the desk wasn't helping as his temper flashed, but he somehow managed to keep it under control. He had hurt Susannah once. The last thing he wanted was to cause trouble for her now. So he would say nothing, regardless of how much the man annoyed him. There was little he could do to make amends to Susannah, but at least he could do this.

Several days had passed, and although Susannah was pleased with the effect Toby's presence had on his children, she still couldn't entirely dismiss the implication of James Keim's words. Were other people coming to similar conclusions about her and Toby? She'd hate to think so.

Mary Keim was staying after school to help every day, and Susannah suspected she had orders to report to her father everything that was said. Still, the girl seemed to be responding to the small responsibilities Susannah gave her, and when Mary relaxed, she had a nice way with the children.

Susannah drew her buggy to a halt at the back porch of Becky's home and tried to dismiss the worries from her mind. It was time for the monthly get-together of the girls who'd been in her *rumspringa* group, an occasion for eating, talking and much laughter. She knew these girls as well as she knew anyone, and with them, she could relax and be herself. Even the fact that she was teaching many of their children didn't seem to disrupt their bond.

Giving her buggy horse a final pat, she headed inside, already hearing the buzz of women's voices, interrupted by laughter. They were all married with children, happy for an evening away from responsibilities, eager to chatter about everything that had happened in Pine Creek since they'd last met.

Susannah paused, her hand on the door. What were the chances they'd heard about Keim's outrage over finding her working alone in the schoolroom with only a child to chaperone them? She shivered, as if a cold snowflake had landed on her.

With an annoyed shake of her head, Susannah opened the door. She would not let herself start imagining things. She stepped inside and was engulfed in a wave of warmth and welcome.

Over the supper Becky had prepared, the talk stayed general, and Susannah was able to join in the chatter about Christmas plans and holiday baking. She glanced around the table at the smiling faces. The eight of them hadn't changed all that much since their younger days, had they?

Sara Esch caught her eye. "What are you thinking that makes you smile so, Susannah?"

"*Ach,* she must be smiling because Toby Unger is back in town." Silence fell after Sally Ann's comment. She'd always had a gift for blurting out what other people might think but not say.

"No, I was remembering the day we snuck off and had our picture taken. Sally Ann, you were so nervous you dropped your share of the money three or four times."

Sally Ann grinned, her good nature never letting her take offense when teased. "I was imagining the bunch of us getting hauled in front of the church to confess. I was sure my parents would have a fit if they found out."

"It was pretty hard to keep them from finding out." Rachel Mast commented, sensible as always. "After all, there *was* the photo."

It had been a fad for a time among Amish teens to have a professional photo made of their group during *rumspringa,* before any of them joined the church. The practice was frowned on by the older folks but generally accepted as part of growing up.

"*Ach,* the boys did far worse than that during their *rumspringa,*" Becky said. "They were no doubt glad that was all the mischief we got up to." She rose from the table and moved to the oak cabinet against the wall, opening a drawer. "And here it is. We were a pretty good-looking bunch, ain't so?" She passed the picture around the table.

"I don't think we've changed all that much," Susannah said, accepting the picture. She glanced down at the smiling faces.

The photographer had taken the picture of the group in a park, arranging the eight of them in various positions on and around a weathered picnic table. She'd thought it odd at the time, and it was only later that she realized what an artist he had been.

The eight of them looked so much more natural than they would have lined up in a row. She studied their youthful faces. They'd all been eighteen then.

Her gaze was arrested by her own face gravely smiling back at her, and her heart gave an odd thud. She'd said they hadn't changed much, but the face of the younger Susannah had had a sweetness and an innocence that she wouldn't find if she looked in the mirror now. She'd been a girl then, looking forward to marriage, secure in Toby's love. She handed the photo on to the next person, happy not to spend any more time staring at her younger self.

Rachel pushed her empty pie plate away, sighing. "The *kinder* seem happy to have two new students in the school. Although from what I hear from Simon, young William is a bit of a handful."

"Just like his *daadi* was." Sally Ann grinned. "Remember when he put a whoopie pie on the teacher's chair and she sat on it?"

The resulting laughter had a slightly nervous edge, as if her friends weren't sure how she'd react to mentions of her old love.

Well, she had to let them see that it didn't bother her in

the least. "Luckily for me, William hasn't thought of that trick. I just hope nobody mentions it to him."

"We won't tell," Becky said. "More *snitz* pie, anyone?" She held the knife poised over yet another dried-apple pie, but she didn't get any takers.

"So I hear Toby is spending a lot of time at the schoolhouse." Sally Ann's blue eyes twinkled, but there was an edge to her voice. Clearly there had been talk.

Well, maybe she could use the Amish grapevine to her advantage. "Toby's *kinder* are finding it difficult to adjust to losing their mother and then moving to a new place. I thought it would help them feel more comfortable if their *daad* was around for a week or so, and helping with the Christmas program seemed a perfect way of doing so."

There was a general murmur of approval. Good. The reason for Toby's presence would be passed along, and hopefully, other people would be equally understanding.

"And it gives the two of you time together, too, ain't so?" Sally Ann was irrepressible. "Take advantage of it, and you might have Toby falling for you all over again."

Susannah's smile froze. Several women started up their chatter again, obviously thinking Sally Ann had gone too far this time.

It wasn't malicious, Susannah knew, glancing at Sally Ann's ruddy, cheerful face. But it hurt, anyway, and the way her stomach was twisting made her think she shouldn't have had that last piece of dried-apple pie.

Which was worse—to have people thinking, like Keim, that she was acting improperly? Or to have them assume she was trying to snare Toby into marriage again?

Chapter Five

After a week of having Toby working at the schoolhouse every afternoon, Susannah had begun to feel that all her fretting had been foolish. Whatever the girls from her *rumspringa* gang thought, she hadn't noticed that people were gossiping about her and Toby.

The previous day, during Sunday worship and the simple lunch served afterward, she'd been on alert for any hint of interest. But she hadn't intercepted any knowing glances or been asked any awkward questions. Surely, if folks were gossiping, she'd have sensed something.

Susannah forced her attention back to her younger scholars, who were rehearsing their part in the program. Apart from an inability to hold up their battery-powered candles and recite their lines at the same time, they were improving. As was Mary Keim, who was directing them. To Susannah's surprise, Mary had come through, once she was trusted with the responsibility for a task.

The *kinder* came to the end of their recitation, and Mary glanced anxiously at Susannah.

"*Gut* work, all of you." There were grins and waving of candles at her words. "Now put your candles in the box on the desk. It's almost time to go home."

As the young ones hurried to obey, Susannah touched

Mary's shoulder. "You are doing very well with the young ones. I'm pleased with your work."

Mary's thin face flushed with pleasure. "*Denke,* Teacher Susannah." She hesitated for a moment. "I…I just try to do what I think you would."

The words touched her. "That's how we learn, ain't so? Keep this up and you can be a *gut* teacher, if that's what you want."

The girl looked away. "I'm not sure," she muttered. Before Susannah could respond, Mary scurried away to help the younger ones with boots and jackets.

Now, what was that about? Perhaps Mary didn't share her father's intent for her, although despite her earlier doubts, Susannah felt that the girl had begun to show an aptitude for teaching.

When Mary opened the schoolhouse door, Susannah saw a light snow was falling. She had to smile at the children's reactions. They walked sedately at first, double file, across the narrow porch and down the steps as they'd been taught. When they reached the ground, they erupted like young foals, prancing and running delightedly through the white flakes.

Mary pulled on her own jacket, looking as eager as the *kinder.* "I'll go out and watch until they're picked up."

"*Denke,* Mary." Susannah closed the door after the girl, shutting out the chill December air, and then had to open it again as Anna came scurrying from the cloakroom with the twins, always the last to get their coats on.

"We're going to make a snowman," Anna announced. "Will you come and look at it when we're done, Teacher Susannah?"

"I surely will," she said, doubting that they'd have time to finish before Becky came to collect her daughters.

She closed the door again and realized that Toby was watching her, a tentative smile on his lips.

"Anna is doing better, ain't so?" He seemed to want re-assurance, as any worried father would.

"Much better." Susannah touched the last of the tall can-dles he'd been constructing with the older boys. A coat of paint and they'd be ready. "She put her hand in the air this morning when I asked for volunteers to read aloud. That's real progress from the first few days, when I couldn't get her to say anything."

Toby's expression eased. "You've been wonderful *gut* with her, Susannah. *Denke.*"

"It's my job." Yet she couldn't help sharing his pleasure. "As for William…"

Toby's eyes darkened. "What has he done now?"

"Nothing so bad." She hastened to assure him. "A few scuffles on the playground, that's all."

"I was afraid of that." Toby's shoulders hunched, and for a moment, he looked like an older version of his son. "I was hoping you'd be able to get through to him. I'm certain sure not doing it."

The bitterness in his voice shook her. "I'm sorry, Toby. You and he seemed to be talking while you were working together. I prayed things were better."

Toby shrugged, running his hand down the plywood candle. "Sometimes we start talking like we used to. But then it's as if William puts a wall up between us." His jaw tightened. "He's my own son, and I can't reach him."

Susannah longed to deny it, but she'd seen it for her-self. William was holding his father at arm's length, and she didn't have a guess as to why. Pity stirred in her heart.

"When did things change between you and William?" The question might seem prying, but if Toby wanted her help, she had to ask it, even if it touched on the subject of his wife.

Toby frowned. "It's related to Emma's death. It must

be. He's older, so he understood a little better what was happening."

Her heart twisted. "*Ach,* Toby, you couldn't protect him from the pain of his mother's dying, no matter how much you wanted to." Any more than he could control his own grief at the loss of his wife.

An unexpected rush of resentment washed over her, and Susannah was horrified. Toby had jilted her and married another woman, and now he expected her to help him deal with the aftermath of her death. She shouldn't let the resentment have sway—it was unkind and unchristian.

Toby swung away from her with an abrupt movement. "Sorry." His voice roughened with emotion. "I shouldn't be talking about Emma, not to you, of all people."

Shame engulfed Susannah. How could she think of herself in the face of his grief and that of his children?

A prayer formed in her thoughts. *Father God, forgive me. Give me a heart clean of pain and jealousy so that I can help them.*

She drew in a long, steadying breath. Then she reached out to touch his arm. "Toby, don't think that. You can talk to me. No matter what else happened between us, we have been friends from the cradle. You can tell me anything." Her fingers tightened on his arm. *"Anything."*

For a long moment she thought he wouldn't respond. Then his gaze met hers, and she felt as if his expression eased just a little. "*Ach,* how many mistakes I've made in my life. Mistakes other people had to pay for." He shook his head, as if trying to shake off the pain. "William... I'm afraid that somehow William felt I didn't love his *mammi* the way I should."

Susannah tried to absorb the impact of his words. That was the last thing she'd expected to hear. Hadn't Emma been the love he'd been looking for when he'd left Pine Creek?

"I don't understand." She took a breath, knowing she needed to hear the truth. "Is William right?"

Toby's jaw tightened. "You thought I left because of you, ain't so?"

She could only nod, bewildered.

For a long moment, Toby was silent. Then he spoke. "I should have told you this years ago. You deserved to hear the truth from me, and instead I ran away." He grasped the plywood candle so hard that his knuckles whitened. "I panicked, that's the truth of it. The closer our wedding came, the more it seemed to me that I was missing out on something." He frowned down at his hands. "I don't even know what I expected to find. I longed to experience something more than Pine Creek—to see other places, meet other people."

She felt the sudden urge to shake him. "Toby, you could have told me. Don't you know I would have understood? I would have given you whatever time you needed."

His lips twisted. "I could always be honest with you, Susannah. I know. I didn't want to face it. I was ashamed to tell you—to see the hurt in your face."

He sounded almost angry. At himself? At her? She wasn't sure, and she'd always thought she could read his every mood. He'd been feeling all these emotions, and she'd never even had a hint of it at the time. Had she been too busy filling her dower chest and giggling with her girl-friends at the time?

She tried to zero in on what was important now. "We were young, maybe too young. We both made mistakes. The *kinder* are what's important now."

He nodded, seeming to look past her at something she couldn't see. "At first all I could think after I went West was how different everything was. There were all these people, and I hadn't known them from the day I was born. Everyone was a mystery to me. Including Emma."

"You loved her." Susannah willed her voice to be steady.

"I fell in love." His lips twisted in a wry smile. "That's how it felt. I had grown into love with you, but with Emma it was more like falling from the barn roof and landing with a thud. So we got married, and then I realized that we hardly knew each other at all."

"You were married." That was the important thing. The Amish married for life, not like the English world, where people seemed to change mates as often as they changed clothes.

"We tried. I think Emma was happy. But then she got sick. It should have brought us closer together, but it didn't."

She knew, without his putting it into words, what he felt. Guilt. He accused himself of not loving Emma enough, and her dying made his guilt all the heavier.

"Toby—"

He cut her off with a sharp movement of his hand. "William was devoted to his *mammi*. Nothing has been right between us since she died."

"I'm sorry, Toby." Focus on the child, she ordered herself. "Have you talked to William about his mother?"

"I've tried." Anger flashed in his face, and she suspected he was glad to feel it after opening his soul to her. "I've tried so many times. But William won't talk about it. He's slipping away, and I can't seem to hold on to him."

She couldn't be angry with him when she knew the depth of his pain. "I understand. We'll keep trying, ain't so? It will get better." The words sounded as hollow to her as they must to him.

"*Ach,* Susannah, you sound as if I'm one of the *kinder,* coming to you with a scraped knee." His tone was harsh. "This is big and real, and you tell me it will get better."

Her own anger spurted up. "What else can I say, Toby?

You have to have hope. There's no magic answer. Just keep loving William, that's all."

He swung toward her, grasping her wrists. "You…" Whatever he was going to say seemed to get lost as his eyes met hers. She could feel her pulse pounding against his palms.

"Susannah," his voice deepened. "I'm such a fool, spilling all this to you. You ought to tell me to go away and solve my own problems."

"I couldn't do that." She tried to smile but failed.

"No." Everything changed in an instant. His gaze was so intense it seemed to heat her skin, and the very air around them was heavy with emotion. "You couldn't." He focused on her lips, and her breath caught in her throat.

She couldn't breathe, couldn't think, couldn't speak. She could only wait for his lips to find hers.

His kiss was tentative at first. Gentle, then growing more intense as her lips softened under his. His hands slid up her arms, and he drew her closer. She was sinking into him, unable to feel anything but his strong arms, his warm lips—

Then the schoolroom door flew open, letting in a blast of cold air. Toby let go of her so abruptly she nearly staggered. She turned toward the door.

Mary stood there, her face scarlet. Her mouth worked, but no words came out. She took a backward step and pulled the door shut with a bang.

Susannah could only stand there, aghast. Of all the things that could happen…

"I've done it again." Toby's mouth twisted as if the words had a bitter taste. "I've messed up your life again, haven't I?"

"Don't," she said quickly. "It's no more your fault than mine. I'll talk to Mary. I'll explain."

But how exactly was she going to explain being caught

in an embrace in her own schoolroom? She was afraid she'd just handed James Keim all the ammunition he'd need to get rid of her.

Chapter Six

Toby strode across the narrow schoolhouse porch and down the steps, almost without seeing them. What had he been thinking? How had he let that kiss happen?

Susannah had deserved to hear the reason he'd left her before their wedding, pitiful as it was. At least maybe now she wouldn't go on thinking it was her fault. It had been his, with his longing to see more of the world. Not that that hadn't been wrong, but when he'd let his needs hurt others, it had been. He'd acted as if all that was important had been his happiness.

The church was right to teach that happiness wasn't the goal of life. The goal was to live in obedience to God, with happiness or sorrow coming to everyone at one time or another.

Well, he'd certainly brought Susannah an added measure of sorrow she didn't deserve. If only Mary could be persuaded not to speak about what she'd seen...

That was probably a futile hope, but he ought to try. Mary was standing by the swings, and she turned away when he approached.

"Mary." He kept his tone gentle. "Please let me speak to you for a moment."

Seeing him, William and Anna came hurrying over.

"*Daadi,* listen." William tugged on his coat. "I have an idea for the program."

"Wait, William." That came out more sharply than he'd intended, and he softened his tone. "Go over to the buggy and wait for me. I'll be there in a minute."

"But, *Daadi,* listen." William was nothing if not persistent, and Mary had taken several steps away already. In a moment he would lose her.

"Now, William." He pointed to the buggy.

William's small face set, but he went, closely followed by Anna.

"Please, Mary, wait."

She stopped, looking like a bird arrested in flight. Her face was turned away from him, but he caught a glimpse of red cheeks. For sure she'd be embarrassed.

"About what you saw…" He fumbled for words. "It wasn't Teacher Susannah's fault. It was mine. I'm to blame. I don't want her to lose her job over it."

Mary had to know what he was asking her, but she gave no sign that she understood. He took a step closer, searching for words that might make a difference. But then Mary fled, running across the snow-covered schoolyard to the shed, where her buggy horse was stabled with Susannah's.

Too late. He wouldn't have another chance. Approaching Mary again would just make things worse. Frustrated, he stalked toward his own buggy.

Anna and William were perched on the seat, a wool lap robe pulled over them. He swung himself up and took hold of the lines.

He sent one last glance toward the schoolhouse. It went against the grain to drive off and leave Susannah there alone and upset. But anything he said or did now wouldn't help. He clucked to the horse.

The icy lane crunched under the buggy wheels, and the mare tossed her head, as if expressing her opinion of the cold. The children sat silent under the lap robe. He turned onto the paved road, the mare's hooves striking the black-top, already cleared of snow by the cars that had gone by.

Toby made an effort to shake loose the worry that pressed on him. There was no point in making the *kinder* think something was wrong. If the worst happened, they'd know soon enough.

"It's looking like Christmas, ain't so?" He nodded toward the spruce trees along the road, their deep green branches weighed down with a coating of white.

William didn't respond, but Anna nodded. "*Grossmammi* said she would make a batch of *pfefferneuse*. Do you think she'd let me help her?"

"I think she'd be very pleased to have a fine helper like you."

Anna's smile lit her face, and she gave a little nod. "*Gut*. I want to take some to Teacher Susannah."

His heart lurched at the mention of Susannah, but he managed to smile. "She'll like it, that's certain sure."

William squirmed. "Move over, Anna. You're taking up the whole seat."

"Am not," Anna retorted. "You are."

Glad as he was to hear Anna standing up for herself, the seat of a moving buggy wasn't the right place for a scuffle.

"Stop it, both of you." They turned into the farm lane, the mare's steps quickening as the barn came into view. "We're almost there."

"She's hogging the seat." William gave his sister a shove.

Anna cried out, slipping from the seat. Dropping the lines, Toby grabbed her, pulling her to safety. The mare, feeling the lines go slack, picked up her pace, and for a moment, Toby had his hands full holding on to his daughter and groping for the lines. Finally he found them and pulled up.

"Hush, Anna. You're fine." He snuggled her against him and focused on William. "What is wrong with you? Your sister could have fallen under the buggy wheels."

William hunched forward, not looking at him. "She's not hurt."

"No thanks to you. You're big enough to know better than to act that way in a moving buggy. I'm ashamed of you."

"You're always ashamed of me." William flared up so quickly, it was as if he'd set a match to dry tinder. "You wish you didn't have to be bothered with me."

"That's nonsense." Toby pulled in a breath. This wasn't the time for anger. "You are my son, William. It's not a bother to be with you. Why do you think I'm helping with the Christmas program if not to spend more time with you?"

"Not me." William's face twisted. "You want to be with Teacher Susannah."

It was like being hit in the stomach. For a minute Toby couldn't catch his breath. Before he could speak, William jumped down from the buggy and took off, running toward the barn.

Toby could only stare after him and feel the taste of failure sour in his soul.

Susannah's first instinct when she'd left the school had been to flee to Becky. She had to talk to someone about what had just happened. She couldn't talk to *Mamm* and *Daad* about it, at least not until she had to.

Despite Becky's reputation as a chatterbox, Susannah knew she could trust Becky to keep silent when it was something really important. She couldn't count the number of secrets they'd shared over the years.

But now, sitting in Becky's warm kitchen, she couldn't seem to find the words to begin. Fortunately, Becky didn't

find anything strange about Susannah stopping by after
school. Smiling, she set a mug of hot chocolate in front
of Susannah.

"That's what we need on a snowy day, ain't so?" She
sat down opposite her. "Did you see the greens we brought
in?"

Susannah nodded, hoping her smile looked natural.
"How could I help it? You have all the windowsills deco-
rated. It looks so nice."

Becky nodded, smiling in satisfaction at the greens and
candles on the kitchen windowsill. A few red berries from
the winterberry bush had been tucked around the pine, too,
making a daring spot of color.

"After the last time we went to town, the twins were
asking why we don't have Christmas trees. I explained
that we want to keep our Christmas centered on God's
gift of Jesus, and I think they understand. But I thought it
wouldn't hurt to do a little more with the decor this year.
And we set up the *putz* in the living room, too."

The *putz,* or manger scene, was an old tradition in Pennsylvania Dutch homes, including those of some Amish.
The children told the Christmas story over and over with
the figures.

"They told me all about it when they got to school
today." She hesitated, thinking of how the school day had
ended. Maybe she was wrong to burden Becky with her
problems. Becky had warned her, but she hadn't listened.

Becky reached across to touch her fingers. "Susannah,
what is it? I can see that something is wrong, and here you
are, letting me babble away about evergreens."

"I don't..." Susannah stopped before she could deny
it, knowing her voice was already shaking. "*Ach,* Becky,
I am in such trouble."

"*Komm* now." Becky clasped both her hands warmly.
"It can't be that bad, can it? Tell me what is wrong."

She spoke as if she were talking to one of the twins, and Susannah was reminded of Toby's anger when he said she was speaking to him as if he were a child.

She took a deep breath. Best just to say it, and quickly. "After school let out, Mary went outside with the *kinder*. Toby and I were alone in the schoolroom."

Becky drew in a sharp breath, as if knowing worse was coming, but she didn't speak.

"We were talking about how William and Anna are doing. He is worried about William, saying the boy doesn't talk to him. He thinks it has to do with Emma's death."

"He shouldn't be talking to you about the woman he married after he left you," Becky declared. "It's not right."

"That doesn't matter. And it's important, if it helps me understand William and find a way to help him."

Becky snorted. "Are you sure it's not Toby you're trying to help?"

"It's the same thing," she said. "If something is wrong between William and his father, it affects both of them."

"I suppose." Becky sounded reluctant to admit it. "Goodness knows it's a hard thing for a child to lose a mother at that age."

"It is," she said softly, remembering Toby's words about not loving Emma as he should. "But we started talking about what happened when he left, and I guess maybe we touched those feelings we used to have for each other." She tried to swallow the lump in her throat. "Anyway we...we kissed."

"*Ach,* Susannah, how could you be so foolish?" Becky's voice was loving and scolding at the same time. "Isn't it enough that he broke your heart once?"

"That isn't the worst of it. Mary Keim came back in. She saw us."

"Oh, no." Becky's fingers tightened on hers, and Susannah could see her mind scrambling from one possibility to another. "I suppose there's no hope that she won't tell her father."

"I don't think so." Susannah rubbed her forehead with her free hand, trying to will away the tension that had gathered there. "Word will get out. It always does."

"I'm so sorry. Didn't I tell you to stay away from him? Now look what he's done. You'd think he'd be satisfied with jilting you once, and now, here he's back again, causing more problems. Kissing you as if you were teenagers again."

It hadn't been the tentative kiss of a teenager, but it was probably best not to admit it to Becky. "It's not only Toby's fault. I'm a grown woman. It's just as much my responsibility. I should never have put myself in that position."

"And it wouldn't have happened if you'd listened to me," Becky declared, indignant all over again. "I hate to say I told you so, but…"

"Go ahead, you can say it if you want." Worst of all, she couldn't really bring herself to regret that kiss. Maybe she was destined to be a *maidal,* an old maid, but that didn't mean she hadn't yearned for Toby's kiss.

"Well, there's no point in crying over spilled milk." Becky seemed to have lost her urge to repeat her strictures once Susannah had told her she should. "We have to think what to do next."

Susannah spread her hands in a gesture of helplessness. "I don't see that there's anything I can do. I doubt Mary will be able to keep from telling her father what she saw."

"Maybe, but you can't just lie down and die. You have to fight." Becky's eyes flashed, and her hot chocolate sloshed dangerously when she pounded the table. "You have to start talking to folks, getting them on your side before Keim can sway them. After all, people here have known you since you were born. They'll listen to you."

True enough. But... "Becky, I can't turn the school-house into a battleground. That is not right."

"It can't be wrong to defend yourself," Becky retorted. "Besides, you'd be doing it for the *kinder.* They need you. Think where they'd be with Mary Keim for a teacher."

"Mary's not as bad as we thought," she murmured. "Anyway, it might not come to that. But I can't start campaigning against James Keim."

Becky frowned. "Well, then, the least you can do is make sure Toby isn't spending time at the schoolhouse any longer. Maybe then the talk will die down."

"How can I do that? How would I explain it to the scholars? It would look as if he'd done something wrong. It might make things worse between Toby and his children."

"Well, if you don't, Toby Unger is going to destroy your life again," Becky snapped.

Susannah could only stare at her for a moment, her lips twisting wryly. "You agree with Toby, then. That's exactly what he said."

Chapter Seven

As soon as her scholars filed into the schoolroom the next morning, Susannah knew that the news of her misdeed had spread. The younger children seemed unaware of anything different, but several of the older boys refused to meet her eyes, and she heard embarrassed giggling from the girls.

"Settle down and take your seats, please." She frowned toward the older ones, and they slid into the desks, making it clear that some of those desks were empty. Susannah quickly checked the row of seats. All of the Keim children were missing, including Mary, who had been coming regularly to help.

Well, that made a statement, didn't it? How many other families would be following their example by tomorrow?

Wrenching her mind into its normal track, she began the day's routine with a reminder of upcoming events. "Don't forget that tomorrow we'll have a final rehearsal for the Christmas program. I expect all of you to be letter-perfect in your parts."

"*Ja,* Teacher Susannah," they chorused in unison.

Tomorrow was the last rehearsal, and Thursday, the Christmas program. After that, school would close for a two-week winter break. If she could just keep going until then, she'd have breathing space to make a decision about the future. Surely she'd have that much time.

She walked slowly between the desks of the first graders, checking as they printed the alphabet. Each child looked up at her with a smile as she passed, and her heart filled with joy. Surely it wasn't God's will that she lose her role here.

Somehow she got through the morning, but it seemed a very long time until the *kinder* were settled with their lunches and a gentle hum of conversation buzzed through the room. Susannah walked into the small back room, which was a combination storage room and coat room. She was taking her lunch down from the shelf when she heard a tapping at the back door.

Her heart gave a little lurch, but when she opened the door, it wasn't Toby. It was Mary Keim, her face red from the cold.

"Mary, you look frozen." She grasped the girl's hands and pulled her inside. *"Was ist letz?"*

"Shh." Mary sent an anguished glance toward the classroom. "I can't let anyone see me," she whispered.

"But you're chilled through. You must come in and stand by the stove."

Mary quickly shook her head. "It's nothing. I had to walk so *Daadi* wouldn't know I was coming."

"Ach, no." Susannah put her arm around the girl. "You shouldn't have."

"I had to." Mary turned away for a moment and then swung back, clutching Susannah's hand. "I had to tell you. I'm so sorry." Tears spurted from her eyes, and her voice shook. "I didn't want to talk. I meant to keep it secret. But *Daadi* saw that something was wrong, and he kept asking me and asking me. He always knows when we're hiding something. I'm sorry. But I told him about you and Toby Unger."

"*Ach,* Mary, don't be upset." How could she blame the girl? She was the one who had done wrong. "I would never want you to get into trouble with your father because of me."

Mary sniffled and wiped away tears with the back of her hand. "I can't stay, but I didn't feel right, not speaking to you myself. And there's something else. I heard *Daadi* talking. He's called a meeting of the school board for Friday. I'm afraid he…"

She let that trail off, but Susannah knew what she was going to say. Keim was going to press for her dismissal. Friday. Well, at least she'd present her last Christmas program before she was told to leave. She drew in a deep, calming breath.

"Listen to me, Mary. None of this is your fault. I don't want you to blame yourself." She touched the girl's shoulder. "You have the makings of a *gut* teacher, if that's what you want to be. But don't let anyone push you into something you don't care about."

Mary looked away from her, and they both knew how unlikely it was that Mary would hold out against her father's wishes.

The girl stared down at the floor. "I wish I was strong, like you. But I'm not."

Susannah didn't feel particularly strong at the moment. Still, it was nice to know someone thought she was.

"I think you'd better go now, before your *daad* realizes you've left." She squeezed Mary's hands. "*Denke,* Mary. Don't worry too much. Whatever happens, it's God's will."

Nodding, Mary buttoned her jacket and pulled her bonnet into place, tying it securely against the wind. She looked for a moment as if she would say something more. Then she shook her head, blinking back tears, and scurried out.

Susannah grabbed the broom and swept out the snow

Mary had tracked in. She was just closing the door again when she heard someone behind her.

"Who was that?" William stood in the classroom doorway, his face tight.

She looked at him steadily for a moment. "Is that the proper way to speak to your teacher, William Unger?"

He flushed, looking down at his shoes. "No, Teacher Susannah. I just… I thought maybe it was my daad."

"Your *daad* never comes in this door," she said. "I'm sure he'll come in the front like always when he arrives to help. Why?"

William shrugged. "Nothing."

Susannah studied the face that was so like Toby's had been at that age. "Is something wrong, William?"

He shrugged again, not answering.

"Because if there is something wrong, you can tell me. Or even better, talk to your *daadi* about it."

He looked up then, his blue eyes filled with misery. "I can't."

Susannah longed to pull the boy into her arms, but instinct told her that would be the wrong course of action. Something was troubling the boy, and if it was something involving his father, she shouldn't interfere. Still, she had to do something.

Susannah touched William's chin, tipping his face up so that she could see it. "Whatever is wrong, you can trust your father. I've known him since he was younger than you are, and I know you can tell him anything. When he comes this afternoon…"

William shook his head abruptly. "I forgot I was s'posed to tell you. He isn't coming today. My *grossmammi* will pick up me and Anna after school."

Susannah felt as if someone had doused her in cold water. Toby wasn't coming. She hadn't realized until that moment how much she'd counted on talking to him.

She straightened, lifting her chin. Very well. She couldn't rely on Toby. She didn't even want to. She would handle this situation on her own.

Mary's words slipped into her mind. *Strong like you.* Never mind that she didn't feel it. A strong woman wouldn't just sit back and let someone take away the job she loved. She'd do something. But what?

"Are you coming to school to help today, *Daadi?*" Anna looked up from her oatmeal on Wednesday morning to pose the question. "Teacher Susannah says we have our last practice today."

Just the mention of Susannah hit Toby like a slap. He'd done enough damage to her for one lifetime. Surely the best thing he could do for her now was to stay away.

"Not today, Anna. I have too much work to do."

Toby glanced at his son. What was William thinking, staring so intently at his wedge of shoofly pie? He'd tried to talk to the boy, but he hadn't gotten anywhere. William seemed to have a talent for avoiding even a direct question. And Toby feared that pressing him too much would make matters worse.

"But *Daadi*..." Anna's small face crumpled. "You have to come. Who will set up the big candles for our program if you don't?"

"I'm sure someone else can do it." He exchanged glances with his mother as she reached across to set the coffeepot on the table. *Maam* was looking about as stoic as William this morning. No doubt she'd heard all about her son's misdeeds already.

"Nobody will do it like you do." Anna was on the verge of tears. "Please, *Daadi.*"

He clenched his teeth. It seemed he was destined to hurt someone no matter what he did.

"Hush, Anna." His mother patted Anna's head. "*Daadi*

and I will both come to help this afternoon. Ain't so, Tobias?" She gave him a challenging look.

Well, at least if his mother was there, that would deflect any gossip. "You're right," he said. "We'll both go."

Once the *kinder* had scurried out into the snow, where his brother waited with the buggy to take them to school, Toby carried his dishes to the sink.

"Denke, Maam."

His mother turned to face him, her lined face stern, her hands clasped together over her apron. It was the pose she always took when she was about to say something you didn't want to hear.

"You're a grown man, Tobias. I don't want to tell you what to do with your life. But I think highly of Susannah."

"I think highly of her, too." His jaw clenched. "I hate that I've done something to hurt her."

His mother winced slightly. "It's true, then. You were seen kissing Susannah in the schoolroom."

"It's true." He felt as if he were ten and about to be sent to *Daad* for a well-deserved spanking. But this was a misdeed that couldn't be resolved so easily. "I never meant it to happen."

"You can't undo it now." Her disappointment in him was obvious. "But I hope you will do whatever you can to mend this situation for her. It's not right that Susannah lose what's most important to her because of you." She might have added "again," but she didn't.

He felt it, anyway. "I know. I will." If only he could think of something that would help.

Toby spent the morning in the shop, working on a carriage, finding some comfort in the craft. It gave him silence and solitude in which to think, but unfortunately that didn't seem to help. He could see no way to undo the trouble he'd brought on Susannah.

By the time he and *Mamm* reached the school that afternoon, the classroom was at the high pitch of excitement that always seemed to accompany the annual Christmas program. His gaze automatically sought out Susannah.

She seemed the same as always, her oval face serene as she tried to keep the *kinder* under control, but he knew her well enough to see the strain in her eyes.

His mother elbowed him. "I'll see if I can help Susannah. You should get the stage set up, ain't so?"

Nodding, he pulled his attention away from Susannah. *Mamm* had it right. He was here to help with the props, nothing else. Enlisting the aid of some of the older boys, he began moving the giant candles into place along the side of the schoolroom.

While he worked, he became aware of the looks some of the older scholars directed at him. So they had heard. Useless to hope they wouldn't, he supposed. But at least they were still in school. As far as he could tell, the Keim children were the only ones who were missing. No doubt James Keim had been very vocal about having his *kinder* in Susannah's school. A totally un-Amish anger gripped Toby, and he had to force it down.

After a few minutes, Toby had all the candles set up in a row, along the side of the schoolroom. They would form a backdrop for the children as they recited. Becky moved along the windows behind the candles, trimming the sills with live greens. She carefully avoided looking at him while she worked, and he was grateful that she'd curbed her outspokenness for the moment. No doubt she was boiling inside with all the things she'd like to say to him.

"Looks *gut,* ain't so?" He clapped the nearest boy on the shoulder and got a grin in return. "We should start setting up the chairs next."

Folding chairs had been borrowed to accommodate all the parents and grandparents who were expected to attend the program. The schoolroom would be overflowing with people by this time tomorrow. At least, he hoped it would. Surely folks wouldn't stay away because of the rumors. The school Christmas program was one of the few opportunities an Amish child had to do something that might be considered performing.

Moving chairs brought him closer to where Susannah stood, directing the placement of the classes on the makeshift stage. He bent to open a chair, not looking at her.

"I'm sorry, Susannah." He kept his voice low, under the clatter of chairs and the sound of the children. "I've brought you trouble, and I never meant to."

"I know." Her voice was cool, her gaze never leaving the *kinder*.

Obviously she didn't want to hear him. He could hardly blame her for that. He went on setting up the chairs, listening to the children reciting as he did. The poems they spoke were typical of Amish school programs, expressing Amish values—humility, faithfulness, meekness, forgiveness.

Forgiveness. Could Susannah forgive him? He didn't know.

He paused, a chair in his hands. No one else was near enough to hear him. This might be his last chance. "I would do anything to make this right," he said quietly. "Anything. I hope you can forgive me."

That brought her gaze to his face. "Don't think that, Toby," she said quickly. "It was as much my responsibility as yours. There is nothing to forgive."

Their eyes met for a long moment. He thought she was speaking the truth—that she wasn't blaming him. But he couldn't excuse himself so easily.

"I want—" His words broke off at a clatter and the sound of raised voices. He swung around in time to see William shove the boy next to him.

"You're in the wrong place. Move over."

"Am not." The boy returned the shove. "You are."

"William," he began. But before he could get the warning out, his son had given the other boy a push that sent him stumbling into the end candle.

It swayed dangerously. He lunged toward it, a warning shout caught in his throat. But he was too late. The candle toppled, hitting the next one. Then, like a row of dominoes, they were all falling, one after another, and the room was filled with the clatter and the squeals of the children as they scrambled out of the way.

Toby reached them in time to catch the last candle and lower it to the floor. Susannah had already waded into the fray, trying to see if anyone was hurt. Then *Mamm* and Becky were there, as well, pulling children away from the mess that had been the stage for Susannah's Christmas program.

"Stop it!" The male voice was loud enough to silence the most high-pitched squeal. James Keim slammed the schoolroom door behind him like a punctuation mark. "What is the meaning of this?"

"An accident..." Susannah began.

"This is not acceptable." Keim didn't wait for her explanation. "I came here today because the bishop urged me to meet with you to resolve our difficulties, and I find the schoolhouse in chaos."

"It's not—" Toby began, but Keim shouted over him.

"Disgraceful!" He glared at Susannah, then the rest of the schoolroom. "The Christmas program is cancelled. The school is closed until a new teacher is hired. You will all go home. Now."

"Wait a minute." The anger that shook him startled Toby. "You can't—"

But Keim was already stomping out the door, as if he had no doubt that his orders would be obeyed.

Hands curling into fists, Toby lunged after him, but Susannah quickly put a restraining hand on his arm.

"Don't, Toby. Don't. It's over." Her voice broke on the words.

All Toby could do was stand there, looking at the despair in her face and know that it was his fault.

Chapter Eight

Susannah struggled to hold herself together. Her students were clustering around her, some of them crying. She had to stay strong for them.

"Hush, now." She drew a couple of weeping children close against her. "There's no reason to cry. It's not your fault."

"We should have behaved better." Zeke Esch, one of her eighth graders, looked at the other children as he spoke. "All of us should." He sent a firm look at William and Thomas, whose quarrel had ignited the trouble.

William studied the tips of his shoes, while Thomas wiped away a tear with his sleeve.

"It startled all of us when the candles fell," Susannah said. She didn't want William and Thomas to be the target of anyone's blame, whatever they'd done. "Right now we must concentrate on cleaning up."

"But, Teacher Susannah, what's going to happen?" Sarah Esch, Zeke's twin sister, had blue eyes bright with tears. "Can't we have our Christmas program?"

Zeke nudged her. "It's worse than that. We're going to lose Teacher Susannah."

There was a fresh outburst of sobs at his words.

Susannah tried to smile, fighting down her own despair

as she looked for the right words. If nothing else, she owed the children honesty, as always. "I'll pray that we can work out this trouble so that I can still be your teacher. But if not, then we must accept it."

And that would be a bitter pill to swallow. How much easier it would be to blame others for this grief.

She had to suck in a breath before she could continue. "If you have a new teacher—"

"No," Sarah said, the word echoed by others.

"If you have a new teacher," Susannah said again firmly, "I know you will behave in a way to make me proud of you."

Several of the older students looked solemn at that, but they nodded.

"Now." She couldn't keep going much longer without breaking into tears. "If you are walking home, you may get your books and your coats and be dismissed. If you are waiting to be picked up, I want you to help with the cleaning."

She glanced at Becky. She looked shaken, but she responded with a quick nod. "Come along now," Becky said, shepherding children away from Susannah. "You heard Teacher Susannah. Sarah, will you help organize the walkers? And, Zeke, you can start that clean-up, ain't so?"

Both of them nodded, looking gratified at being singled out as the oldest scholars in the school. In a moment the *kinder* had moved away reluctantly.

But she'd barely had time to take a breath before Toby appeared, holding William with one hand and Thomas with the other. He gave them each a shake, his face grim.

"What do you have to say to Teacher Susannah?"

"I'm sorry, Teacher Susannah." Thomas couldn't get the words out fast enough, and tears welled in his eyes. "I shouldn't have done it."

"*Denke,* Thomas." She touched his shoulder lightly,

and Toby let him go. He scurried off, obviously eager to disappear.

Toby gave his son another little shake. "Well, William?"

"Sorry," William muttered, his gaze on the floor.

She could see that Toby wasn't satisfied with the apology, and she shook her head in silent warning. It might only make the boy's behavior worse to push the point.

"*Denke,* William." She said the words quietly, hoping he'd look at her.

But he didn't. He wrenched himself free of his father's grip and darted off.

Muttering something, Toby started to go after him, but she caught his arm.

"Let him go. Talk to him later, after you both calm down. And listen to him."

"It hasn't done too much good so far," he said. "As if I haven't done enough harm to you, and my own son—"

"Don't, Toby." She really couldn't listen to any more. "Just get him and Thomas to help clean up. That's the best thing right now."

He gave a curt nod and stalked off to help clear away the mess.

It seemed to take forever, but the schoolroom was finally neat again. And empty, with all the children gone. Susannah stood for a moment, looking around, trying to create a picture in her mind of the schoolroom as it looked at this moment. If she never saw it again—

Stop, she ordered herself. Moving stiffly, she went to her desk and sank down on the chair. Maybe she should take her personal belongings home with her, just in case, but she couldn't seem to summon the energy to do so. She felt empty. Drained. All she wanted was to be home, with the door closed, free to indulge in the tears that kept threatening to overflow.

The schoolroom door opened, and she barely had time

to put her defenses in place before Toby had come in. He strode toward her with the air of a man who'd made up his mind about something.

"Susannah, we have to talk." He planted his hands on her desk.

"Not now." She pushed herself to her feet, feeling as if she was weighed down by a heavy load. "Later."

"This can't wait." His lips twisted. "What happened is my fault. I have to do something."

She couldn't cope with his feelings, not when she could barely manage her own. "There's nothing you can do." *Please, Toby, go away and leave me alone.*

"There has to be. If I hadn't given in to impulse and kissed you, you wouldn't be at risk of losing your school."

Her heart winced at his casual mention of their kiss. She could never let him know how much it had affected her. "We were both to blame."

He shook his head, jaw set, brows lowering, making her think how little he'd changed from the boy she'd loved. "No."

"You were always impulsive," she said. "And always sorry afterward, too."

He stared at her for a moment and then, quite suddenly, he smiled.

The smile traveled straight to her heart, bursting there like fireworks and illuminating all the dark corners.

He caught her hands in a typically impulsive movement. "Marry me, Susannah," he said. "I know it doesn't solve all your problems, but at least then you wouldn't have to worry about teaching or dealing with a man like Keim." He seemed to warm to his theme even as she struggled to process it. "Think about it. We have always been friends. We could have a good life together, couldn't we?"

His hands tightened on her fingers, and in that moment,

she saw two things very clearly. She had never stopped loving him. And she couldn't marry him.

Her breath caught in her throat. Perhaps a few weeks ago she'd have said yes. She'd have taken what he offered her, thinking half a loaf was better than none.

But not now. If this trouble had taught her anything, it was that she was stronger than she'd thought. She would not take second place in anyone's heart, not even Toby's.

"No." She said it with a finality she hoped he'd recognize, and she pulled her hands free. "I can't take that way out of my troubles, Toby." She walked away quickly before he could stop her. "Losing my job is not a good enough reason to marry you." She grabbed her coat and hurried out the door.

"Wouldn't you like a little piece of shoofly pie?" Susannah's mother hovered over her, a plate in her hand. She had been forcing food on her ever since Susannah got home from school the previous day. She'd eaten something to please *Mamm,* though even her mother's delicious baking tasted like ashes in her mouth.

"Leave the girl alone," her father said, correctly interpreting her expression. "Eli will have a piece. He's always hungry."

The family, gathered around the kitchen table, smiled at the reference to her next older brother's notorious appetite. Eli grinned.

"Give it here, *Mamm.* I'll have Susannah's share." He accompanied the words with a wink, reminding her of their childhood, when the two of them had always paired up against their two older brothers.

She tried to smile, but her face felt stiff. Much as she appreciated the support they'd come to offer, she longed for nothing more than to be left alone to nurse her wounds.

That was a useless hope, she knew. In the close-knit

Amish community, there was no such thing as struggling with your problems alone.

Becky, who'd shown up before her brothers, refilled coffee cups around the table before sitting down next to Susannah. "What are we going to do?" she said, resuming the discussion that had been interrupted by *Mamm*'s determination to feed all of them. "We certain sure don't want our *kinder* taught by anyone but Susannah. Maybe the other school board members—"

"I spoke to them already," *Daad* said. At Susannah's look of surprise, he nodded. "Went over to see them last night, that's what I did." He frowned. "They want to support our Susannah, but it's no use expecting much from them. Harley Fisher works for Keim, after all, and Matthew Busch is too ill to get into a wrangle."

"Well, I still say we should go to the school board meeting," her oldest brother insisted. "Make Keim come right out in the open with his accusations."

Susannah shuddered at the thought, thinking of what Keim was likely to say. Still, was there anyone in the church who hadn't heard it already? Her already-sore heart twisted.

"I say we go to Keim's house and have it out with him," Eli said, his eyes bright and his big hands curling into fists. "He's got no right to dictate to the rest of the church. And maybe we should have a talk with Toby while we're at it."

Daad reached across the table to clasp Susannah's hand in his, an unusual demonstration of affection for someone usually so taciturn. "What do you think, Susannah? You know how we feel about this, but it's for you to say."

She looked around the table, and the love and caring in each face eased her pain. She glanced at the candles and greens *Mamm* had placed on the windowsills and thought of her scholars' faces, and the answer seemed to grow clearer.

"*Denke*. It helps so much to know you care. But how can we do something that could divide the church? It would be a poor way of honoring the birthday of the Prince of Peace."

They objected to the idea of giving in so readily, of course, but fortunately before they could wear Susannah down with their arguments, there was a knock at the door.

Eli, who was closest, rose to answer it and drew back to usher in John Stoltzfus, the bishop. The clatter of voices ceased abruptly at the imposing figure.

Bishop John was tall and lean, stooped a little after years of bending over in his work as a farrier. His beard was more white than gray, but his eyes were still bright with the energy needed for the two church districts under his care.

"*Wilkom,* Bishop John." *Daad* eyed him warily, but there was nothing very frightening in the bishop's expression. He smiled and greeted everyone, and when his keen eyes rested on Susannah, she felt as if he looked right through her and still found reason to smile.

"We should have a little talk, ain't so, Susannah?"

She nodded. There was bustling around the table as everyone found some reason to be elsewhere. In a few minutes, with warm hugs and murmurs of support, they were gone, leaving her alone to talk with Bishop John.

He pulled a chair over so that they sat facing each other, and she gave him a quick, apprehensive glance before lowering her gaze to her hands, folded in her lap.

"There's no reason that I know of for you to look so worried," Bishop John said, his deep voice gentle. "I didn't come with two ministers to confront you with wrongdoing. It's *chust* the two of us, wanting to talk about the problem."

Susannah blinked back a rush of weak, foolish tears. "*Denke,* Bishop John." She took a steadying breath. "I don't know what to do."

"That is a *gut* place to start," he said, and she thought she detected a trace of amusement in his voice. "Too many folks think they already know what the Lord wants them to do."

She risked a glance. "James Keim says I have given the board cause for dismissal."

"*Ja,* I have heard from James. What do *you* say?"

Of course Keim would have gone straight to the bishop with his accusations. She should have anticipated it. "I was wrong to let Toby kiss me in the schoolhouse. That was inappropriate, and I don't blame anyone for being shocked. But the problem at the rehearsal for the Christmas program—"

Her voice shook a little as she remembered that scene. "It was an issue with two boys misbehaving, and I would have dealt with it as I have with countless problems in the past ten years. There was no good reason to cancel the Christmas program and disappoint the students and their families."

"I should tell you I have talked to Toby Unger," he said. "He is very quick to blame himself for what happened between you. He says that he took you by surprise, and he is truly grieved that he's caused you such trouble."

She was shaken at the thought of Toby discussing her with the bishop, and her cheeks flamed. Naturally the bishop would put this incident first, concerned as he was with the hearts and souls of his people.

"The guilt belongs to both of us," she said firmly. "I'm a grown woman, not a foolish teenager, and I am…was… the teacher."

"True, the schoolhouse is not the place for kissing." Slight amusement sounded in his voice. "But there is not anything wrong with a kiss between a single man and a single woman that I know of. Toby tells me he has asked you to marry him."

Her hands clenched. "I have told him no." She could feel the bishop's gaze on her face, and she didn't dare look up.

"Do you love him, child?"

She felt her cheeks grow hot. She might try to lie to herself, but she certain sure couldn't lie to the spiritual leader of the church.

"I do love him," she said softly. "I always have. But he... he doesn't feel the same way toward me."

To her relief, Bishop John didn't pursue it further. "As to this other matter, my feeling is that James Keim acted in haste." He paused, and Susannah could almost feel him choosing his words. "I will continue to pray for guidance, and I'll speak to James again." He didn't sound as if he expected much from that conversation.

"*Denke,* Bishop John. I'm grateful." She met his gaze then and saw the sorrow there. Bishop John truly lived the command to bear one another's burdens, and she could almost see them weighing on his shoulders.

"If nothing else," he said, "I think the Willow Run School will need a teacher next fall. I'll speak with them. I'm sure they would be eager to have you."

"*Denke,*" she said again. "It's very *gut* of you."

So why didn't she feel more joy at the thought of having a school again? The truth sank in. Losing her school was a terrible thing.

But losing Toby was even worse.

Chapter Nine

Stretching out next to the carriage he'd been working on, Toby squirmed his way underneath to check the axles. The owner had complained of a squeaking noise he hadn't been able to account for, so he'd brought it back to the workshop, probably hoping Toby's father would be fit for work again. Well, he'd have to settle for Toby.

Even Toby's persistence in keeping busy hadn't been enough to keep his mind occupied. Bishop John had accepted his version of things without much comment, other than to say that he'd be seeing both Keim and Susannah and hoped to straighten matters out. But so far Toby hadn't heard anything else. Nearly twenty-four hours had passed since Toby had stood with Susannah in the schoolroom and watched the destruction of her dreams.

He frowned absently at the axle just above his face. A dozen times he'd nearly gone over to the Miller place to try to speak to Susannah, but what could he say that hadn't already been said?

Again and again he saw Susannah's face when he'd suggested marriage. He could kick himself. No wonder she'd refused him. She'd known it was an impulse of a moment.

If only Bishop John succeeded with Keim...

The shop door opened, letting in a blast of cold air and

a flurry of snowflakes. It closed again quickly, and he recognized William's shoes and pants He stiffened. He still hadn't gotten a satisfactory explanation of William's actions. He seemed to hear Susannah's voice telling him to keep trying, to be as calm and patient as she always was.

"I'm under here, William."

William bent over, peering beneath the carriage, his face inverted. "Can I come under, too, *Daadi?*"

Toby patted the floorboards next to him in answer. In a moment William had rolled under the carriage and moved next to him, staring into the underbelly of the vehicle.

"What are you doing?"

"The owner says it's making a funny noise, so I'm trying to figure out why. I thought it might be the axle, but the fittings are fine." He patted the sturdy axle just above his face.

"What else could it be?"

Toby suspected William hadn't come out to the shop in the snow just to ask him questions about the buggy business, but if it helped ease him into what he wanted to say, that was okay by him.

"I'm thinking, maybe the springs." He indicated them with the pliers he held. "They're what give you a comfortable ride, and one of them might be rubbing."

William nodded solemnly. "You like to work with tools, *ja, Daadi?*"

"I do." *Give me the right words for my boy, Father. Help me to find out what troubles him.*

William was silent for a moment. "I liked building the candles with you. I hope they're not broken."

"I hope so, too. But if they are, maybe we can fix them." He breathed another silent prayer. "Most broken things can be fixed, if you know what's wrong with them."

William nodded, his forehead furrowed.

Treading cautiously, he went on. "It seems to me that something's broken between you and me. We're not as close as we used to be."

He paused, but William didn't respond. His gaze was fixed on the springs.

"I don't know why," Toby said. "If I did, maybe I could fix it. Was it something to do with your *mammi*'s dying?"

William's lips pressed together. He shook his head. "Look, *Daadi*. That spring is crooked. Maybe that's making the noise."

Toby's heart sank. But he tried to infuse some enthusiasm into his voice. "I believe you're right. Let's see if I can fix it."

He eased the pliers along the spring, trying to grasp the kink that had formed. It might have to be replaced.

"I heard you," William said suddenly. "You were talking to *Grossdaadi* and *Grossmammi* about sending me and Anna out West with them after *Mammi* died."

Toby's hand jerked, and the twisted spring snapped. He dropped the pliers. He knew perfectly well what conversation William had overheard. He'd thought both children safely asleep when Emma's parents had brought up their idea.

Toby's heart thudded in his ears. He wanted to set William straight, but he'd better try to find out exactly what the boy had been imagining. "What did you think that meant?"

"You wanted to send us away." A tear trickled down William's cheek.

Toby shifted to his side so that he could see his son's face more clearly, his shoulder brushing the axle. "Then I think you didn't hear the beginning of the talk. Or the end. Because if you did, you'd know that it was *Grossmammi* and *Grossdaadi* who brought up the idea. They wanted to take you with them. And you know what I told them?"

William's gaze met his, wide-eyed, and he shook his head.

"I said I knew they wanted to help, but I couldn't even think of being parted from my children. I said I loved you and Anna more than anything, and I couldn't let you go." He looked steadily into his son's eyes. "That's exactly what happened. You can write to them and ask them, if you want."

William just stared at him. Then he rolled right into Toby's arms. Toby squeezed him close, his heart swelling, caught between laughter and tears. What a place for a father-and-son talk!

But at last they had cleared the air between them. What difference did it make where it happened?

William snuggled against him the way he had when he was younger. "I'm sorry, *Daadi*." His voice was muffled. "I'm sorry I was mean to you."

"It's okay. I love you even when you're mean to me."

William sniffled a little. "And I'm sorry I messed up the Christmas program. I shouldn't have got mad at Thomas and pushed him and wrecked the candles we made. We worked so hard on the Christmas program, and I messed it up."

"All of us worked hard on it," he said. The faintest glimmer of an idea seemed to light up Toby's mind. So many people were involved with the program. Maybe, just maybe...

He moved, sliding himself and William across the floor.

"What are we doing?" William seemed to sense his urgency.

"You know how I said that broken things could be fixed? Well, maybe the Christmas program can be fixed, if we all work together."

And maybe, if his idea worked, even more than the Christmas program.

* * *

Everyone in Susannah's family seemed to have some-where to go on Friday afternoon. She wasn't sorry that even her mother had taken off to go shopping, but she was a little surprised *Mamm* hadn't insisted on Susannah accompanying her. Maybe her mother realized Susannah wasn't ready for casual encounters with any church fami-lies yet.

At last she had the solitude she'd been longing for, but oddly enough, she didn't find it as peaceful as she would have expected. She found herself aimlessly wandering around the house, looking for something to do. Each time her thoughts slid toward Toby, she ruthlessly reined them in.

She had been right to turn down his proposal, she told herself firmly. He hadn't really meant it, and a marriage founded on guilt wouldn't stand much chance of happiness.

The Willow Run School was a far better subject for her to concentrate on. She'd been there several times when the local Amish teachers got together for meetings. It was al-ways helpful to share ideas, and Susannah had picked up more than one useful tip that way. The school building was much like the Pine Creek School, with maybe a few more scholars. She'd think of it as a challenge.

All of her teaching materials and books were still at school, of course. She'd been so numb after everything that happened, she hadn't been able to bear the thought of pack-ing them up. Maybe after Christmas, it would be easier.

The whole extended family would be here for Christmas Day, and the following day, Second Christmas, they'd be making the rounds, visiting other relatives. Several gifts were already tucked away in the dower chest in her bed-room, but she was still working on a muffler for her brother Eli. Sitting down in the rocking chair, she took it from the workbasket and smoothed it out across her lap. The variegated brown yarn was soft to the touch but sufficiently masculine, she thought, and the half-double crochet stitch was easy enough that she could do it and carry on a conversation at the same time. In the evenings, she and *Mamm* sat on either side of the lamp to work, their tongues going as fast as their hooks or needles.

Smiling a little, she began a new row. This was better. She hadn't thought about her troubles in at least a minute or two.

Susannah had barely reached the end of the row before she heard a buggy driving in the lane. Sticking the hook into the yarn ball to hold her place, she went to the kitchen window to see who was back already.

But it wasn't any of the family. It was Becky. She stopped by the back porch, jumped down from the buggy and trotted toward the door.

Susannah hurried to open it. "Becky, I wasn't expecting you. I'll put the kettle on."

"No time for that." Becky yanked Susannah's wool jacket from the hook by the back door. *"Komm, schnell."*

Susannah resisted Becky's efforts to push her arm into the sleeve. "I'm not one of the twins. You don't have to dress me. Where are we going in such a hurry?"

"Don't you trust me?" Becky's eyebrows lifted.

"Not when I think you're up to something." Susannah took the jacket firmly into her own hands. "I'm not taking another step until you tell me where we're going."

"All right, stubborn. I'm going with you to get your things at the school. You don't think I'd let you do it by yourself, do you?"

Susannah blinked back a rush of tears. Becky knew her so well. She must have guessed that was preying on her mind.

"That's wonderful kind of you. But we don't have to do it today—"

"Better sooner than later, otherwise you'll just be stewing about it."

"I'm not stewing."

"You're moping then, and that's worse. *Komm.* We'll get it over with, and if you want to have a good cry, no one will see you."

Susannah recognized the look in Becky's eyes. She was determined, and when Becky was determined, she wouldn't let you have a moment's peace until you did what she wanted. Susannah might as well get it over with.

"All right. We'll go." Susannah pulled on the jacket. "But only because I know you'll nag me to death if I refuse."

Though she didn't relish the purpose of the expedition, Susannah found her spirits lifting a bit once the buggy was moving down the road. The crisp air seemed to blow away the cobwebs in her mind, and sunlight sparkled on the snow-covered fields where ice had formed.

Becky gave her a searching glance. "So, how are you, really?"

Susannah shrugged. "Better, I guess. I'm starting to feel enthusiastic about teaching at a new school. And I do need my materials so I can sort through them, if nothing else. Maybe it is best just to clear my things out of the Pine Creek School." She tried not to let her voice quaver on the words.

"I'm sorry." Becky's voice mirrored her grief. "I know how hard this is. That school has been your life."

True enough. Odd, that the school had fulfilled her all these years, and yet now, she longed for more. But the gift she wanted wasn't going to be hers.

"I'll miss the school. The memories. The children." She made an effort to swallow the lump in her throat. "But I can move on. Really. Now that the worst has happened, I can deal with it."

"I never doubted it for a minute," Becky said. "But what about…well, Toby? I know you'd probably rather not talk about him, but he did ask you to marry him."

For once Susannah couldn't tell from Becky's voice what she was thinking, and the brim of her black bonnet hid her face. "He asked me," she admitted. "And I refused him."

"But—"

Susannah shook her head and hurried on. "It wouldn't be right. Toby doesn't care for me that way, not anymore, and I…I guess I'd rather be a good teacher than somebody's second-choice wife."

"You're sure about that?" Becky turned a concerned face toward her as they approached the turnoff for the school.

Susannah nodded. "It's for the best. All of this has made me realize that I truly have forgiven what happened between us. I can let it go and trust that God has a plan for my life."

"I'm sure the *gut* Lord does have a plan." Becky negotiated the turn into the school lane, where the snow was banked high on either side by the snowplow. "But you know, maybe Toby is part of that plan. And if he is, don't let your pride stand in the way."

Susannah was still trying to adjust to that startling statement when she saw something equally surprising. The lane was lined on either side with buggies, all the way up to the schoolhouse, where still more ringed the building, giving it the air of being surrounded.

Her stomach clenched. "Becky, what's going on? If there's going to be a school board meeting, I don't want to have anything to do with it."

Becky ignored her, driving the buggy straight up to the door. "It's not the school board meeting. It's your scholars. They have a surprise for you."

Susannah gripped the edge of the buggy seat. "I don't want any more surprises."

"Now, don't be foolish," Becky chided. "You can't disappoint the *kinder*. Look, here's Eli to take you in."

Sure enough, her brother was already reaching up to seize her waist and swing her down before she could find words to refuse.

"Just come along," Eli said. "There's nothing to worry about."

Becky had already slid down, and she grasped her other arm. "That's right." Together they propelled Susannah across the porch and into the school.

Chapter Ten

Susannah's mind seemed to stop working for an instant when she walked inside her classroom. The room was filled with people—so many it seemed the walls would burst from the pressure. Family, neighbors, Bishop John, parents and former students, so many of the scholars who had gone through the Pine Creek School in the past decade. And everyone was smiling.

Eli and Becky swept her up to her own desk chair, pushed her into it and turned her to face the makeshift stage at the side of the room. It was then that she saw her students, lined up in front of the tall candles Toby had made. The metallic gold paint that formed the flames of the candles seemed to glow, but not more than the faces of the children…the boys in their black pants, white shirts and suspenders, the girls with pristine white aprons over a colorful array of dresses.

Suddenly the room grew still. Not missing a beat, her scholars spoke together. "*Wilkom,* Teacher Susannah."

She could only smile at them, her eyes misted with tears, as her heart swelled in her chest. For this moment, at least, she was at home.

Mary Keim stepped forward, her smile seeming perfectly confident. With a quick glance at Bishop John, she spoke.

"We *wilkom* all of you, our dear visitors, to the Pine Creek School, for our Christmas program." She turned, nodded, and the children moved quickly and quietly to their places. Mary slid into a chair placed at the side of the stage, probably so she could prompt anyone who forgot a line, and the program began.

It was her own program, of course, with every word familiar to her, and yet it seemed to Susannah that it had taken on a special dimension. It was hard to imagine Mary taking control, standing up in front of everyone and looking so composed. She had found the strength she'd been seeking.

But how had Mary dared to go against her father this way? Surely James Keim didn't support this idea after he'd expressly forbidden the Christmas program.

Susannah took a quick glance around the room, searching for Keim, and found him standing at the back corner, his arms crossed over his chest, his expression forbidding. No, he didn't look as if he'd changed his opinion.

The first graders came forward, grouped nervously close together, with the twins and Anna holding hands. Their recitation was a simple poem wishing everyone a merry Christmas, and they made it through without a single glance at Mary for help. They closed by inviting everyone to join them in singing Jingle Bells, and the resounding chorus seemed likely to lift the roof off.

Songs, poems, recitations, skits were done, interspersed with the singing of familiar Christmas carols. The morals were the simple ones that were reiterated year after year in Amish school programs, celebrating the gift of love, the joy of giving, the humility of the believer honoring the birth of Jesus, the Light of the World. Susannah glanced around as the program moved forward, seeing the rapt faces, the pleased smiles, some apprehension when a child began and the glow when he or she finished.

Some things never changed. Most of the people in this room would have heard every one of these thoughts expressed at countless Christmas programs, and yet, like the Christmas story itself, they were fresh and new each year.

The final presentation involved ten students with lighted candles—a process that always filled Susannah with lively apprehension. Becky and Mary moved quickly along the row of children, lighting the white candles they held.

The poem began, with the ten lights symbolizing ten young Christians. As the words were recited that showed how each one fell short from his or her Christian duty, a flame was extinguished, until only one was left—the one held by young William. His solemn face was pale in the light of his candle as he held it firmly. The rest of the scholars gathered behind him as they spoke of how one person could shine his light so that it reached the world and brought others to Christ. Then William, intent on his task, went to each child, lighting the candles one by one until the room was aglow with their light.

Mary's voice lifted in the first line of "This Little Light of Mine," and the children soon joined in. Susannah suspected there wasn't a dry eye in the room by then. As they reached the end of the song, they lifted their candles so that the light spilled out over the whole room.

Zeke, the oldest of the scholars, stepped forward.

"We just want to add one more thought to our program before it ends. Teacher Susannah has been a light to us.

We don't want to lose her." He sent a challenging look around the room.

For an instant there was silence. Then the schoolroom erupted with the sound of applause and murmurs of agreement that became louder and louder.

Bishop John stepped out to stand by the children. "*Denke.* We thank you, boys and girls, for showing us so much today. I think we all agree that we don't want to lose Teacher Susannah because of a foolish misunderstanding." He looked directly at James Keim.

Susannah's breath caught. It was the public confrontation she'd longed to avoid, and yet it had been accomplished in such a lovely and loving way. How would Keim respond?

James Keim stood stiffly, hands at his sides. His gaze was locked with that of the bishop. Susannah found she was holding her breath.

At last Keim nodded. "I agree. It was a misunderstanding."

Thank you, Lord. Susannah's heart filled.

The room began to hum with excited conversation. Mothers started uncovering the trays of cookies and cakes set out on a long table at the back of the room. And Susannah's students rushed to her and enveloped her in their love.

It was nearly an hour until the schoolhouse emptied enough that Susannah could look for answers to the questions that bubbled through her mind. She found Mary Keim in the midst of taking down Christmas decorations.

"That can wait until later." She caught Mary's arm before she could climb up on the step stool. "Tell me how this came about. I couldn't believe my eyes when I saw you standing up there leading the *kinder*."

Mary flushed. "I could hardly believe it myself. But it was important to the little ones, ain't so?"

"I'm sure it was." She still felt a little overwhelmed at the love her scholars had showered on her. "But your father..." She let the question die out, not sure she wanted to know if Mary had openly defied her parents.

"It was the bishop," Mary said, a smile lurking in her eyes. "Bishop John came to the house and talked about how important the Christmas program was to the whole community. And when he asked me to help right in front of my *daad,* well, *Daadi* just couldn't say no."

"I guess he couldn't." She had to suppress a chuckle at the thought of that conversation. Bishop John had been wily, it seemed. "So the bishop was the one who thought of all this?"

Mary shrugged. "I guess. Anyway, he's the one who spoke to us." She hesitated, and then she went on in a rush. "I really wanted to do it. No matter what."

Touched, Susannah patted the girl's arm. "When school starts again, will you be back as my helper?"

Mary flushed again, with pleasure this time. "If you want me."

"That's certain sure." Her first impression of Mary Keim had certainly been mistaken. "You're going to make a fine teacher, if that's what you want."

"More than anything." Again she hesitated. "Teacher Susannah, I hope you can forgive my father. I want to learn from you, not replace you."

"Of course I forgive him." She gave the girl a quick hug. "And who knows? You might end up doing both."

Letting Mary get back to her work, Susannah cornered

Bishop John before he could slip away with the last group of parents and children.

"*Denke,* Bishop John. I don't know how you thought of this, but I'm truly grateful for all the trouble you've gone to for me." She blinked back a fresh set of tears at the thought.

"*Ach,* Susannah, you owe me no thanks. It was important that you know how much we value you, no matter what you decide to do in the future." His eyes crinkled with a smile. "Besides, the idea wasn't mine. This was all Toby Unger's doing. He's the one you must thank."

"Toby?" Her voice shook a little on his name.

Bishop John nodded. "He came to me with it all thought out. Seems he and that boy of his were determined to make things up to you." He gave her a little push. "I think I saw him carrying things into the back room."

Warmth spread through her. No matter how much she regretted losing what might have been between her and Toby, at least she now understood that their friendship was solid and unbreakable, just as it always had been.

Bishop John was right. She owed Toby her thanks, and she'd best do it now, before she lost her nerve.

When she reached the back room, she found Zeke and William helping Toby store the program props on the wall shelves. All three looked around at the sound of her steps.

"Toby, I... May I have a minute?"

Zeke grinned and clapped William on the shoulder. "Let's go grab some cookies. We deserve it after all this work, ain't so?"

William glanced from her to his father, and she thought she read hesitation in his face. Then he nodded, and the two boys headed back into the schoolroom.

When they were alone together, Susannah found herself suddenly tongue-tied. "Toby, I...I... Thank you."

"Forget it." He grinned, and for an instant he was a mischievous boy again. "It wasn't just me. I talked to Bishop John, and then the two of us talked to Becky and your parents, and it just snowballed."

"But it started with you." She took a step closer, her embarrassment slipping away. This was Toby, after all. She had always been able to say anything to him. "We didn't exactly part on the best of terms, and I—"

"Don't, Susannah." A spasm of pain crossed his face, wiping away his smile. "Every chance I get, I just end up making a mistake and hurting you."

"You didn't hurt me by asking me to marry you." She was as close as she dared get to him without risking him seeing how deeply he affected her. "I know that you were only trying to be helpful."

"Helpful." He grimaced. "All I've done is make your life a shambles since I came back, but I never meant for that to happen."

"Toby, I…" She was trying to find the words that would reassure him when his hands shot out and grasped her arms. His warmth penetrated the fabric, heating her skin, and her mouth went dry.

"Whatever else you might think, at least know that I meant it when I said our friendship was a solid foundation for marriage." His grip tightened. "But that's not all, and I didn't even realize it until I thought I'd cost you everything."

He took a step closer, and her heart was beating up in her throat so hard that she couldn't have spoken to save her life.

"I know you, Susannah Miller. I know you better than I've ever known anyone else in my life. The more I see of you, the better I understand. You're honest and good all the way through. No matter how I tried to kid myself, I know now that you have always held first place in my heart. I love you, Susannah. I always have, and I always will."

The rapid rush of words stopped, and he looked at her with his heart in his eyes. He lifted her hands, holding them close to his lips, so that she felt his warm breath on them when he spoke again.

"What about it? Do you think you could possibly take a chance on me again?"

Susannah was caught between laughter and tears. "*Ach,* Toby, you know me so well. Can you possibly doubt the answer to that question?"

Relief seemed to wash over his face. She knew he really had been uncertain, and her heart leaped. She raised their clasped hands so that she could touch his lips with her fingertips.

"I know we're in the schoolhouse," she said softly. "But I think this occasion merits a kiss, don't you?"

She could feel his smile as his lips claimed hers, and then she was lost in the warmth and tenderness and belonging that bound them one to the other. She slipped her arms around him, holding him close. *This time, forever.* The words seemed to form in her mind. Despite all the grief and pain, they'd found their way back where they belonged.

A thought hit her, and she drew away an inch or two. "We mustn't rush. The *kinder*... We have to think of them. We must give them time to get used to the idea."

Toby nodded. "We will, but I think they won't find it hard." A smile tugged at his lips. "Maybe, by the time you're ready to quit teaching for a family of your own, you'll have Mary trained to step into your place."

Blushing at the thought of the children they might have together, she nodded. If he was right about William and

Anna, this really might have been her last Christmas program as teacher at the Pine Creek School.

But whether it was or not, she knew for certain what her future Christmases would be like. She and Toby would be celebrating together for the rest of their lives. As the children had said in their program, love was the best Christmas gift of all.

* * * * *

A PLAIN HOLIDAY

Patricia Davids

It is with heartfelt love that I dedicate this story to my brothers, Greg, Bob, Mark and Gary. I'm sorry for the grief I gave you as your spoiled-brat sister. You guys made me tough. You taught me to throw a ball like a boy and not like a girl, and you allowed me to share many adventures. Thanks for that and for your lifelong love and support. Merry Christmas, from Sis.

And suddenly there was with the angel a
multitude of the heavenly host praising God,
and saying, Glory to God in the highest,
and on earth peace, good will toward men.
—*Luke* 2:13–14

Chapter One

"This is the worst Christmas ever."

Sally Yoder bit the corner of her lip and glanced over her shoulder at her young charge. She shouldn't have said that aloud. It made her sound ungrateful. She wasn't. She was happy to have a good job as a nanny for the Higgins family. Most days.

Eleven-year-old Kimi wasn't paying attention so Sally stared out the window again. In her hand, she held the most recent letter from her mother. It had arrived last week. Sally kept it in her pocket and took it out whenever she was missing home. Like now.

Traffic clogged the street below her employer's Cincinnati apartment building. It was rush hour, although she saw scores of cars no matter what time of day she looked out. The view was cold and depressing. The holiday lights and Christmas decorations didn't improve it much. Piles of dirty snow lay melting into gray slush along the sidewalks where pedestrians wove in and out of the mess as they hurried along.

Sally's upbringing among the serene Amish farms in Hope Springs, Ohio, had ill-prepared her for the noisy bustle of life in the city.

This is my rumspringa, *my time to experience the out-*

side world and discover if I wish to remain Amish. I should be eager to see and do everything here in the Englisch *world.*

But she wasn't, and she knew why. It was hard to enjoy the adventure when her heart remained in Hope Springs. Rather, the broken bits of it remained behind, scattered at Ben Lapp's feet. It was awful to love someone who didn't love her back.

She glanced at her letter again. It wasn't possible to be more homesick than she was at this second. She reached for the ties of her Amish prayer *kapp*. She often twirled the ribbon around her fingers when she was deep in thought, but she realized her head was bare. She had been dressing English for three months now and it still felt odd. Would she ever put a *kapp* on again?

"If I don't get a new iPod, it *will* be the worst Christmas ever." Kimi proved she had heard Sally's comment, after all. Kimi was sprawled on her bed with her smartphone, that ever-present accessory, clutched in her hands. It giggled and shouted "Text message!" in a cartoon voice that Sally found increasingly irritating.

It was the first day of winter vacation for Kimi's private school. The girl had been complaining all morning about missing her friends and being bored.

Kimi suddenly sat bolt upright. "Jen got blue diamond earrings from her stepdad? No way. That is so awesome. I should let Grams know I want a pair. She likes to buy me cool stuff." Kimi flipped her long black hair out of her face and began typing furiously on her phone.

"Christmas is not about expensive gifts." Sally used her stern "nanny voice" to deliver the message.

"Whatever."

Sally shook her head and returned to contemplating the dreary world outside. If Kimi were this materialistic at eleven, what would she be like as an adult? The answer was easy. She would be like her mother.

Michele Higgins rarely had time for her children. Shopping and lunch with her friends took up most of her day. Sally was just the latest in a long string of nannies to raise the children. The family's money came from the huge real estate business Michele's workaholic husband managed. The contrast between this family and Sally's simple Amish roots was glaring.

"Christmas is about our Savior's birth. It is a time to reflect on our salvation. A time to give thanks for the blessings God has bestowed on us. A time to visit family and friends who are dear to us."

"I don't know how you people live without electricity. I'm so glad my grandmother left the Amish when she married Grandpa McIntyre. Ugh! How can Christmas be fun without shopping and holiday lights?"

"The beauty of the season doesn't come from lights and store displays. We enjoy going to see them in town, but God decorates the land in His own way this time of year. The snow lies like a pristine white blanket over the Amish farms and countryside. Sometimes, the snow glitters so brightly in the sun that it hurts my eyes, but it's so beautiful that I can't stop looking."

"Okay, it's pretty, but what do you do for fun?"

"Many things. At Christmastime, my mother's kitchen is filled with the smell of wonderful baking things. The youngest *kinder,* my brothers and sisters, will start pestering *Mamm* to make her delicious peach cobbler with snow ice cream. Someone will host a cookie exchange and my married sisters will come over and help *Mamm* bake all day."

"Sounds like work."

"*Nee,* it's not. The kitchen is full of laughter and happy

chatter. We have such good times together." And she was going to miss it all this year.

"What's a cookie exchange?" Kimi asked, while at the same time answering a text, leaving Sally to wonder how she could do two things at once.

"A cookie exchange is a kind of party. Each family that's invited will bring a big container, sometimes even a bucket, filled with all kinds of cookies and baked goods. The hosting family has hot chocolate, coffee and cider for everyone. There's sure to be singing and game playing and lots of cookie sampling. Then, when it's time to go home, each family fills their bucket with everyone else's delicious baked goods to enjoy all week long."

"Sounds boring. No wonder you left." Kimi plopped on her stomach to read another text message.

Sally's spirits plunged. A Plain Christmas was the best kind of Christmas, but she might never be a part of one again. She was at a crossroads in her life. For a long time she had been wondering if she truly belonged among the simple, devout people. She didn't possess a meek spirit, and she couldn't pretend any longer that she did.

She turned her mother's letter over to read the back. With all the news her mother relayed, Sally found herself reading the same small tidbit again and again and wishing there was more. Some of the ink was blurred where her tears had fallen on the paper.

We heard Ben Lapp has taken a job at the McIntyre horse farm and likes working there. His mother says he'll be home for Christmas though.

Ben would be home, but Sally wouldn't. She was here to get over him, but it didn't seem to be working.

Kimi had caught Sally crying the day the letter arrived. In a moment of weakness, Sally had told her why. Kimi's advice was to go out and buy something nice. At her age, Kimi couldn't understand that material things didn't mend hearts.

The door to Kimi's room burst open, startling Sally into dropping her letter. Ryder, Kimi's younger brother, came charging in. "You'll never guess what," he shouted.

Kimi slapped her phone facedown on the bed. "Can't you learn to knock, you idiot!"

Sally scowled at her. "Don't call your *bruder* names."

"It's pronounced *brother,* and tell him he should knock."

Ryder rolled his eyes. "If I knocked, you'd just tell me to go away. Guess what?"

Ryder, an eight-year-old bundle of energy, was Sally's secret favorite. Maybe it was because they shared the same red hair and overabundance of freckles. His parents had placed him in a special program for hyperactive children. Because of that, he only went to school in the mornings. He and Sally spent every afternoon alone together and they both enjoyed it.

Kimi sat up cross-legged on the bed. "Okay, I'll guess your news. Mom and Dad have decided it's better for me to be an only child so they're giving you to a needy family for Christmas."

Sally crossed the room and snatched up the phone. "I'm keeping this."

Kimi's mouth dropped open. "Why?"

"That was a mean thing to say. Until you apologize to your...brother...I keep the phone."

"Oh, for real!" Kimi crossed her arms and glared at Sally.

Smiling, Sally slid the phone in the pocket of her jeans.

Kimi caved. "This is so unfair. I'm sorry...*bruder.*"

"That was not a sincere apology." The girl's imitation of Sally's Amish accent didn't offend her. It made her more homesick. She picked up her mother's letter.

Kimi huffed and threw herself back against her headboard.

Ryder held his hands wide. "Doesn't anyone want to hear my news?"

"I do," Sally said.

"Dad's taking Mom to Paris for Christmas."

Kimi screamed and leaped off the bed. "We're going to Paris?"

Ryder dropped his hands to his sides. "You didn't let me finish. Dad is taking Mom to Paris and we are going to Grandma's. Yay!"

Kimi's face fell, but brightened again quickly. "New York isn't Paris, but it's still better than Cincinnati. Grams will take me shopping at all the best places."

Ryder folded his arms, a gloating expression on his face. "Not that grandmother, Kimi-Ninny. We're going to Ohio to spend Christmas vacation with Grandma McIntyre on her farm."

"No! Not there!" Sally said.

The two children turned shocked faces toward her. She quickly recovered her composure and tried to look unaffected. "I mean, I'm sure you'll have a wonderful time."

"On a horse farm in the middle of nowhere? Not likely," Kimi snapped.

Ryder tipped his head to the side. "I know why Kimi doesn't want to spend Christmas with Grandma McIntyre, but why don't you? I thought the Amish liked horses."

"I want to experience a non-Amish Christmas in the city. I'll talk to your mother about it. I don't think I'll be needed."

Kimi looked at Sally with an odd expression. "Grandma McIntyre broke her leg last week. She can't keep an eye on Ryder, and I'm not going to babysit him for two weeks."

Sally pressed her lips together tightly. What did God have planned for her? Not to be the wife of Ben Lapp, that was sure and certain. So why was He sending her to the very place where Ben had a job?

"Did you know our grandmother used to be Amish?" Ryder asked.

Sally smiled at the boy. "I do. My father is a contractor. He built the new stables on your grandmother's farm. That's how I learned your mother was looking for a nanny. Your grandmother put in a good word for me and I got the job." Sally hoped her odd reaction would soon be forgotten.

A malicious gleam sprang to Kimi's eyes. "I know why you don't want to go. It's because *he* is there."

Sally closed her eyes. She would never share another confidence with Kimi. No matter how lonely she was or how much she needed to confide in someone.

"Who are you talking about?" Ryder asked.

Kimi's grin bordered on evil. She held out her hand. "His name starts with a *B*. Shall I tell my blabbermouth brother more, or can I have my phone back?"

"The grandbrats are coming for the entire Christmas break. Somebody shoot me now."

Ben Lapp smiled at Trent's gloomy tone and continued brushing the mare he had just finished exercising. Trent Duffy, the head groom at the McIntyre Stables, had a way of making any little problem sound dire. "Mrs. McIntyre will be happy to have her grandbabies here for the holidays."

"I'm not talking about her son Sam's kids. I'm talking about her daughter Michele's two brats."

Ben fumbled and dropped his brush in the straw.

Sally Yoder worked as a nanny for Michele Higgins. She wouldn't come along on a Christmas family gathering, would she? Surely not.

Snatching up the brush, he checked to see if Trent had noticed his reaction. Trent was busy unwrapping Lady

Brandywine's front legs. Ben resumed his work. "So the whole family is coming. That's nice."

"No, Michele and her *über*-rich husband are going to Paris. Just the kids and their nanny are staying. Hey, didn't I hear the nanny is a friend of yours?"

Ben closed his eyes and bowed his head. Sally Yoder had managed to make his life miserable for two solid years. "*Nee,* she's not a friend."

"That's right. She left the Amish or something, and now she is shunned or whatever you people call it."

Ben ran the brush along the mare's sleek brown neck. "Sally is not shunned. She never took the vows of baptism. She is free to choose the *Englisch* life. I've known her since the first grade, but we're not friends."

"Englisch?"

"It means English. What we call people who aren't Amish."

"Someday you'll have to explain to me about the shunning stuff. Would you hand me that curry comb?"

Ben stopped brushing and slipped under his horse's neck to hand the metal comb to Trent. Maybe he could arrange to be gone while Sally was here. Mrs. McIntyre had been good about giving him time off in the past for weddings and such. The loss of salary would be a small price to pay to avoid seeing Sally. "When did you say they were coming?"

Trent looked out the open stable doors. "If I'm not mistaken, that's their car pulling up to the house now."

Ben's faint hope evaporated. So much for making his escape. Still, the McIntyre horse farm was a good-sized facility. He could stay out of sight if he tried.

Trent led his horse to her stall and closed the lower half of the door. "They'll want help carrying in the luggage. Michele won't lift anything heavier than a hundred dollar bill. Must be nice to have all the money in the world."

"I'll finish up here for you," Ben offered.

"No way. I'm not going to be the only one getting yelled at for scuffing her expensive bags. Come on."

Ben looked out the stable doors toward the black SUV parked in the drive. A woman with bright blond hair, a fur-trimmed coat and tall leather boots got out of the driver's seat. A boy about eight charged out from the backseat and came running toward the stable.

"Ryder, get back here," his mother yelled. He stopped. Ben could see the indecision on his face.

A young woman in jeans and a short leather jacket with a long braid of fiery red hair hanging over her shoulder got out next. She held out her hand to the child. "Ryder, come greet your grandmother first."

Ben looked closer. Dark glasses obscured her face but he knew that voice, and it didn't belong to a woman who looked so...*Englisch*.

The boy ran back to her. "But I want to see the horses, Sally."

"They will still be there after you say hello to your grandmother."

She glanced around the yard. Was she looking for him? Ben stayed where he was. For two long years, Sally Yoder had made a complete fool of herself running after him. She never understood that he wasn't interested. She wasn't the kind of woman he was looking to settle down with. Still, he had been shocked when she took a job in the city.

Trent slapped him on the back. "Let's go. The bags won't get any lighter."

There was no point in putting it off. He would have to endure two weeks of Sally throwing herself at him at every turn, but then she would leave with the family. It wouldn't be fun, but he would manage. He stepped out of the barn and walked toward the car in resignation.

A second, younger girl with black hair got out and stood

huddled against the cold beside her mother. "Please, don't make me stay here. I will die of boredom. Let me come with you."

Her mother patted her cheek. "Your dad and I need some alone time. You'll have a wonderful two weeks with your grandmother."

"No, I won't."

Michele walked toward the house, leaving the children standing beside the car.

Ben approached the group. "Would you like some help with the bags?"

Sally pulled her sunglasses off. The stare she gave him dropped the temperature by ten degrees. "Hello, Ben. Come along, children. Let's get out of this awful weather."

She shepherded the children into the house without a backward glance. Ben watched in stunned surprise as she walked away. Sally hadn't gushed about how glad she was to see him or how much she had missed him. Had she really changed so much? He wouldn't have thought it possible.

How could she go from mooning over him for years to ignoring him?

He honestly hadn't expected her job in the city to last this long. To begin with, he thought she'd left because she hoped he'd realize he couldn't live without her. She was wrong on that score. He enjoyed his Sally-free time. Until today, he thought the only thing that would stop her foolishness for good was for him to marry someone else. Unfortunately, he hadn't found the right woman. Yet. But he sure wasn't going to settle for a wild-spirited redhead with no *demut*.

Sally suffered from a serious lack of humility. When he chose a wife, it would be someone who knew the meaning of meekness and modesty. Someone who didn't question the old ways at every turn and didn't make him feel like a trophy buck in a hunter's sights each time she looked at him.

He pulled a pair of suitcases from the back of the SUV and headed for the front door. He knew what he wanted in a wife and Sally Yoder wasn't it. Somehow, he would avoid her for the next two weeks if he had to hide in the haystacks.

Chapter Two

I can't do this.

Sally caught her lower lip between her teeth to stop it from trembling. She couldn't spend two weeks pretending she didn't care that Ben was here, too. How could she hide her feelings for so long?

"Welcome, everyone, and Merry Christmas." Velda McIntyre, an elegant woman with piercing blue eyes and gray hair cut in a short bob, rolled forward in her wheelchair. She was dressed in a pink jogging suit. A cast covered her left leg from hip to toe.

The Higgins family stood in the large foyer in an awkward group. Sally remained in the background, willing the suddenly shy children to show their grandmother some affection. She heard the door open behind her. She didn't have to look to know it was Ben.

He was the last man on earth she wanted to see. No, he was the only man on earth she wanted to see. She wanted to drink in the sight of him. She wanted to gaze into his beautiful brown eyes and apologize for her abrupt manner outside and for so much more. Instead, she focused on her hostess.

Mrs. McIntyre's face glowed with excitement. She clapped her hands like a child. "I'm so happy to see all of you. We're going to have such a wonderful old-fashioned Christmas. Come here and give me a hug, Ryder. You've grown so much."

"Does your leg hurt?" Ryder inched closer.

"It was silly of me to fall on the ice and break my old bones just before Christmas, wasn't it? It only hurts when I'm not getting a hug from my favorite boy." She held out her arms.

Ryder jumped forward and gave her an enthusiastic squeeze. Kimi, still pouting after two hundred miles, gave her a lukewarm embrace.

The elderly woman didn't seem to notice. "You children have no idea how much fun I have in store for you. We'll bake cookies the way my mother and I did when I was your age, Kimi. We'll make a real gingerbread house, too, and decorate it. Your grandfather always said it wasn't Christmas without one. How does that sound?"

"Totally awesome, Granny." Kimi couldn't have sounded more uninterested if she tried. She didn't want to be here and she didn't care who knew it.

"What do I get to do?" Ryder asked as he leaned on the arm of her chair. For him, a farm was the perfect place to spend Christmas vacation.

"I haven't forgotten about you. You can help with the cookies, too, but I'm giving you a special mission. I'm sending you to find us a Christmas tree. Your sister will go along with you, but you are in charge of finding the perfect one."

Ryder grinned. "I'll find the best one on the lot, Granny."

Mrs. McIntyre hugged him. "You can't find the perfect Christmas tree at a lot, dear. You have to take a sleigh ride up into the forest the way your grandfather and I used to do with your mother. You'll see dozens of trees to choose from, but you will know the perfect one when you spot it.

Trent, you can take them up above Carson Lake tomorrow, can't you?"

He quickly shook his head. "I'm afraid I have too much work to do before the snow moves in, but I can spare Ben for a few hours."

"Will you take them, Ben?" she asked.

"Sure. I'd love to take the kids on a sleigh ride."

Just the sound of his voice brought tears to Sally's eyes. She furiously blinked them back. How pathetic was it to be head over heels for someone who didn't care about her? She studied the large painting of a horse on the wall instead of looking at him. She would just have to get over him.

Please, dear Lord, let it happen soon.

Mrs. McIntyre said, "You will have to cut the tree down with a saw, Ryder. It's hard work, but Ben can help you. He'll lash the tree to the back of the sleigh for the ride home, too. The harness bells sound so merry when you're dashing across the snowy fields. You'll never forget the sound. And on your way back, you will stop and visit my mother. She lives with my two brothers and their wives on a farm a few miles from here. They haven't seen you since you were a baby, Ryder. Mama was so excited when I told her you were coming. She'll have good things to eat and hot tea or cider to warm you before you start home again. I only wish I could come with you."

Sally saw Mrs. McIntyre's eyes mist over. She chanced a glance at Ben. He wore a kindly smile that told her he cared about his employer. Sally had missed his smile. When Ben looked her way, she focused on the painting again. She didn't want him to see how much she still cared.

Going away had been for the best. She was more certain of that now than ever. She didn't have an Amish heart. She tried hard to fool herself and everyone else into believing she belonged among the Plain people, but she always knew she would leave one day when she found the courage.

She had decided to make a play for Ben when she was eighteen because she knew he would never propose to a girl like her. She ran around with the wild group of teens. He stayed on the straight and narrow. She kept up the charade of being madly in love with him to discourage her family and other young men from pressing her to marry. Marriage would bind her to the Amish life forever.

Her plan worked. Until she made the mistake of actually falling for Ben. Soft-spoken, caring, always helpful, he was a wonderful fellow but she had been right. He had no interest in settling down with her. Her plan had one side effect she hadn't counted on. She learned there were several young women in her community who wouldn't go out with Ben because they didn't want to risk hurting her feelings. After making such a fuss about him for so long, she couldn't convince them she had suddenly stopped liking him.

That was when she found the courage to leave.

Ben deserved someone who embraced the Amish faith and way of life wholeheartedly. She wasn't that woman, but she wouldn't stand in the way of his happiness.

"Can we go get the tree now?" Ryder asked.

Mrs. McIntyre laughed. "Settle in your rooms first. Ben will take you tomorrow. Ben is a groom here. He's Amish, Ryder. Do you know what that means?"

"Sure. Sally's Amish, too. They talk funny and only drive horses and buggies. Mom cussed a lot when we got stuck behind a buggy on our way here."

"Not a lot, Mother," Michele said quickly.

Mrs. McIntyre turned her attention to Sally. "You're from the Hope Springs area, too, aren't you? David Yoder's daughter, right? He did a fine job building my new stables. I suspect from the way you're dressed that you're enjoying your *rumspringa.*"

"Yes, ma'am. I'm grateful you told my father about this position and that you vouched for me."

"Your father said you were a fine, upstanding young woman. That was good enough for me."

"I don't know what I would do without you," Michele added quickly.

Mrs. McIntyre looked pleased. "Do you and Ben know each other, Sally?"

"We do." Sally gave him a cool smile. He dropped his gaze to his boots and didn't say anything.

Mrs. McIntyre patted the wheels of her chair. "I'm so grateful you agreed to come along and help me look after the children over Christmas vacation, Sally. We must make sure you get a chance to visit your people while you're in the area."

"I would love that," Sally said eagerly. A visit to her family would cheer her up and get her away from Ben. Maybe she could convince Mrs. McIntyre to let her stay for several days.

Michele stepped to her mother's side and bent to kiss her cheek. "I've got to run. I need to get back and finish packing. Our plane leaves at nine o'clock tonight. Have fun with the children. Sally, I'd like to speak to you outside."

"You're not staying for supper, Michele?" Mrs. McIntyre's face fell.

"Wish I could, really. Merry Christmas, Mom. See you in two weeks. We'll have time to visit then, I promise." Michele kissed Ryder and Kimi on the cheeks and hurried out the door.

Sally glanced at Ben and saw he was watching her. Her heart lightened. His gaze slipped from her head to her shoes and back up again. Slowly. He seemed puzzled by what he saw. Her momentary satisfaction was quickly swallowed by cold reality. He was noticing her *Englisch* clothes with silent disapproval. No, she wasn't the woman for him.

After Sally followed Mrs. Higgins outside, Ben shook his head. How had she changed so much in such a short time?

"Can I go see the horses, now?" Ryder asked.

"After Ben takes your bags to your room," Mrs. Mc-Intyre said. "Do you remember which one it is?"

"I think so. That way, right?" Ryder pointed to the hall leading to the west wing of the house.

"That's right. All the way to the end. Kimi, you and Sally will have the rooms on either side of his."

"Come on, Ben, let's put this stuff away. I want to see the horses." He took off at a run down the hall.

Mrs. McIntyre laughed. "I don't envy Sally trying to keep up with him. He's all go, go, go."

After depositing the luggage in their rooms, Ben followed Ryder outside. Michele was going over a list with Sally. When she saw Ryder, she pushed it into Sally's hands. "You'll figure it out."

"Bye, Mom." Ryder ran past.

"Bye, dear." Michele waved to him. When he was out of earshot, she turned back to Sally. "Make sure the presents are marked from us."

"I will. Have a nice trip."

Michele sighed. "Paris is wonderful, but I do wish they would learn to speak English there. I mean, how hard can it be? You learned Dutch and English."

"Pennsylvania Dutch," Sally replied quietly.

"It's the same difference, isn't it?"

"Almost." Sally's voice slipped lower.

"Pennsylvania Dutch isn't Dutch at all. It's Deitsh, a German dialect," Ben said as he stopped beside them.

Michele curled her lip. "Whatever. Make sure you get everything on the list, Sally."

"Yes, ma'am."

Michele got in the car and sped out of the yard. At least she was allowing the children to visit. Mrs. McIntyre's life hadn't been easy since she lost her husband to cancer. She deserved a chance to share her happy memories with her family and pass on the stories of her youth to her grand-kids. She didn't deserve to be ignored.

Ben held out his hand for the bag Sally was clutching. "May I take that in for you?"

"*Nee.* I've got it."

"Don't let the *greilich Frau* get you down."

"She isn't abominable, and shame on you for saying it." Spinning around, Sally marched toward the house. Her thick, gleaming hip-length braid swayed behind her as if it had a life of its own.

He never expected to see her hair down. Even in a braid. An Amish woman did not display her crowning glory to anyone but God and her husband. It was true that Sally hadn't taken her vows of faith yet, but still, it was a dis-turbing sight, although he wasn't sure why. He'd seen *En-glisch* women with their hair down. None of them made his pulse kick up a notch and his chest tighten until it was hard to take a breath.

What would Sally's hair look like unbound? He imag-ined a riot of fiery red ringlets and curls. It would be beau-tiful. He shook off the thought and shoved his hands deep in the pockets of his coat. It wasn't right to imagine such things.

At least she wasn't dogging his every move. Yet. What was her game this time? He'd find out sooner or later. He glanced toward the corrals where Ryder was climbing the white-board fence. There was someone he might be able to pump for information.

He sauntered up next to the boy and leaned his arms on the top rail. Inside the enclosure, a black horse with a white star pranced and tossed his head. "This fellow is Wyndham's Fancy. He's put in some impressive times on the track. Your grandmother thinks he'll be her next champion."

"He looks like a champion to me. What kind of horse is he?"

"Your grandmother raises Standardbreds, although we have a few ponies to keep some of the more nervous horses company, and a draft horse, too."

"Can I ride this one?"

"I'm afraid not. Wyn loves to pull a sulky, but he doesn't care to have a rider on his back."

"What's a sulky?"

"It's a two-wheeled cart that's used in horse racing. I'll show you one later."

"Can I see more horses?"

"Come this way." Ben led the excited boy toward the new stables. The bright red building was trimmed in white. A central corridor divided the long rows of stalls. The place smelled of horses, hay and oiled harnesses. Ben loved it.

He introduced Ryder to a number of his grandmother's prized animals. When they had made the circuit and were at the last stall, the one that held Dandy, the farm's draft horse, Ben said, "I can see you are excited about spending Christmas on the farm. What about your sister?"

"I think it's tight, but Kimi thinks it's jacked."

Ben chuckled. "Could you *shvetza Englisch,* maybe *ja*?"

"What?"

"Talk English."

Ryder grinned. "I think it's great, but Kimi thinks it's terrible. She hates the farm. She would rather go to Paris with Mom and Dad. Or to New York and stay with our other grandmother."

"Was it Sally's suggestion for you to come here?"

"No. She about fell over when I told her. Kimi said Sally didn't want to come because she didn't want to see some guy she knew was here."

Ben perked up. "Are you sure?"

"I think so. Anyway, Mom said Sally had to come because Grandma can't look after us. I'm glad she came. I really like Sally. Better than any of our other nannies. She's cool. She doesn't think I'm stupid like Mom and Dad and Kimi do."

"You seem pretty sharp to me." Why would anyone call this energetic and charming child stupid?

"Sally says I'm brighter than a kerosene lantern at midnight."

Ben ruffled the boy's hair. "That's bright."

"I wish Mom thought I was smart, but I don't do so good in school."

Ben leaned closer. "I didn't do so well in school, either."

"Honest?"

Ben nodded. "Honest."

"Do you think Sally might marry someone who doesn't do well in school? I mean, if he was older. She's really smart."

It was clear the boy was taken with her. Ben tried to keep a straight face. "If Sally is as smart as you say, I reckon she knows there's more to a man than schooling."

Ryder looked up at Ben in relief. "Good."

"Is she dating anyone?" Ben asked, trying to sound casual.

Ryder shrugged his shoulders. "I don't know."

"Ryder, come in and unpack," Sally called from the doorway of the house.

The boy waved at her and turned to Ben. "I'd better go."

Ben nodded and digested the information Ryder had shared as the boy ran toward the house. Maybe Sally had finally come to her senses. Ben hoped and prayed that was the case. Maybe she was happy in the outside world. She was good for Ryder, that was certain.

Did she have an *Englisch* boyfriend? That would explain her rapid change of heart.

It should have cheered him to think Sally was interested in someone else…but for some odd reason it didn't. At least she seemed content to avoid him, and that was what he wanted.

Wasn't it?

"Are you seriously going to make me ride in a one-horse open sleigh with my pain-in-the-neck brother?" Kimi demanded.

It was early afternoon on the second day of their stay. Sally had managed to avoid Ben after their first meeting but that didn't mean she wasn't thinking about him. She looked out the bedroom window. Ben was already outside getting the sleigh ready for their tree-cutting expedition and the trip to the children's great-grandmother's home. The sky was overcast and it looked as if it could start snowing at any moment.

Sally turned to Kimi and said, "An old-fashioned sleigh ride is fun. Try to enjoy yourself today."

"Old-fashioned is right," Kimi groaned. "Nowadays, we don't think frostbite is fun."

"You won't get frostbite. Not if you dress warmly. Put on extra socks and wear your mittens. Make sure you take a scarf to cover your face. I'll have hot chocolate waiting for you when you get home. How does that sound?"

"Wait. You aren't coming with us? You get to stay here in a warm house and watch TV while poor little Ryder and I are freezing our toes off?"

"Yes."

"That is *so* unfair." Kimi flounced onto the bed.

"What is unfair?" Mrs. McIntyre asked.

Sally turned around. She hadn't heard the wheelchair approaching over the thick carpet. Kimi launched herself off the bed. "It's unfair that Sally doesn't get to join in our fun, Grandma. I know she's dying to come with us today. Tell her it's okay."

Sally shook her head. "I don't care to go along."

Kimi moved to stand beside Sally and slipped an arm around her waist. "She's just saying that. She doesn't want you to think that she's trying to horn in on our fun, but Sally is practically part of the family. I feel terrible about leaving her here."

"Sally, I never meant to exclude you. By all means, accompany the children.

"*Nee,* I couldn't." Sally disengaged Kimi's clinging arm.

Mrs. McIntyre held up one hand. "It's settled. You are going with them, and I don't want to hear another word about it. I'll call the stable and tell Ben to expect one more on this trip. I know my mother will be delighted to have more company."

Sally's halfhearted smile vanished as Mrs. McIntyre rolled away. A whole afternoon with Ben. This would not be good.

Kimi leaned closer and muttered, "If I have to be miserable, you have to be miserable, too."

Sally looked at her sharply. "Why do you hate me so?"

"I don't hate you. I like you." Kimi smiled, as she waltzed out of the room.

Sally stood staring at the empty doorway. *Please, Lord, let Ryder find his tree quickly.*

Chapter Three

"This is her doing. I know it is."

Ben threw a heavy blanket in the back of the sleigh, still fuming after Trent delivered the last-minute news that Sally was joining them. So much for her change of heart.

Trent stood with his arms crossed. "Look on the bright side. You'll have someone to help you watch the brats."

Ben checked the stash of tools in a box fitted behind the backseat. "Why can't she get that I'm not interested in being her *boo-freind*?"

"Her what?"

"Boyfriend," Ben translated. It was harder to speak English when he was upset.

"Have you told her that?" Trent held out a silver thermos of coffee.

Ben took it and shoved it under the front seat. "Not in so many words, but I've made it clear."

"Apparently not."

Maybe Trent was right. Maybe blunt speaking was required. He'd avoided Sally, ignored her at singings and frolics when the younger crowd from their church got together. He'd told others he wasn't interested in courting her, but he hadn't told Sally to her face. He didn't want to hurt her feelings. He'd always liked her, even after she started running with the wilder crowd. But then she started telling her friends he was The One. He had no idea what caused her obsession with him, but enough was enough. He'd find an opportunity to tell her exactly what he thought of her pointless pursuit today.

He walked around the horse, checking to make sure the harness was secure and hitched properly. Dandy, the only draft horse on the farm, shook his cream-colored mane, making the harness bells jingle gaily. Satisfied, Ben checked over the sleigh. Painted a rich, dark mahogany color with yellow pinstriping, the sleigh was as pretty as they came. The two small bench seats in the interior were upholstered in thick tufted burgundy mohair, a material that was both warm and water resistant. A smaller box on runners had been added to the back to enable the estate staff to haul loads of firewood, bales of hay or other equipment when the roads were impassable. It would easily carry a Christmas tree. The sleigh wasn't Trent's preferred method of travel, but Ben was right at home in one.

Trent glanced at the gray sky. "The forecast is calling for snow."

"It's winter, Trent. It snows in the winter." There was already eight inches on the ground. By the end of March, there could be several feet, if not more. Ben wasn't concerned about a little snow. Dandy could plow through just about anything. Besides, if the *kinder* got cold, they'd want to come home more quickly, and he'd be rid of Sally that much faster.

"They're calling for a major storm. It could miss us, but it may move this way. Don't lollygag. Get a tree, visit Grandma Weaver and get back here. I wish Mrs. McIntyre wasn't so set on sending the kids out to get a tree. I know it's because that's what her husband loved to do, but these kids don't care. With you gone, I'll have to clean the stalls myself."

Ben swept his hand toward the driver's seat. "Say the word and I'll shovel manure while you go for a sleigh ride and a few hours of winter fun."

"Not on your life. I'll clean the stalls. You just get back in time to help me exercise those colts."

"Get going. Get a tree. Visit Granny. Get back. That's my plan."

Ben climbed into the sleigh and drove up to the front door to wait for his passengers. He didn't have to wait long. The front door burst open, and Ryder came flying out. He skidded to a stop when Ben held up one hand. "You can't come without a hat and mittens."

"It's not that cold."

Ben pointed to his own flat-topped, wide-brimmed black felt hat. "It's not that cold...yet. In an hour, you'll be telling a different story. Covering your head will keep you twice as warm as just a coat and that's a fact."

"Ryder, come put your hat and gloves on," Sally called from inside the doorway.

Ryder sighed. "Sally says the same thing. She always makes me button up and put a hat on, even if I'm not cold."

"We're not going anywhere till you are dressed properly." Ben was pleased to hear Sally looked after the boy so well. She had always been good with children.

Ryder charged back the way he'd come. He seemed to have two speeds. Fast and faster.

When he came out a moment later, he had his hat and mittens in his hands. "Can I sit up front with you, Ben?"

"Sure."

"Can I drive? What's your horse's name? Is it a long ways to the trees? How are we going to cut the tree down when we find the perfect one?"

"Put a sock in it," Kimi said as she came out the door and climbed in. "I don't want to listen to your endless questions this whole stupid trip. It was bad enough on the drive here yesterday."

Ryder stuck his tongue out at her, but fell silent. Ben smothered a grin. He had siblings, too. They didn't always get along, although they loved each other dearly. He looked forward to going home and seeing all of them on Christmas Day but Christmas was still a week away.

Sally came out with Mrs. McIntyre, who waved to them all. "Have fun. Give my mother and my brothers all my love."

"We will, Grandma!" Ryder waved wildly.

Sally kept her gaze down as she approached the sleigh. She was dressed in jeans, tall boots and a long black wool coat, the same style as his mother wore. Serviceable and sensible, a good Amish coat. Not like the short brown leather jacket she had on yesterday. She settled a red-and-white stocking cap on her head and wrapped a red-and-white-striped knitted scarf around her neck. The bold colors were not ones an Amish woman would choose.

Her clothes were a contradiction that mirrored Ben's confusion about her. Was she still Amish? Did she intend to return home after her *rumspringa,* or was she determined to become a fancy *Englisch* woman? If that was the case, he had nothing to worry about. As an *Englischer,* she was forbidden to him and she knew it.

Pulling on matching mittens, she paused beside Ben. "I'm sorry about this. Mrs. McIntyre insisted I join you."

She spoke so softly that he could barely hear her. Was she trying to make him think she hadn't planned this? Should he believe her? He wanted to give her the benefit of the doubt, but he hesitated. He'd never known her to tell an outright lie, but Sally could bend the truth to suit herself. Especially where he was concerned.

After she got settled in the seat behind him, Ben flicked the reins to get Dandy moving. When they were out in an open pasture, he handed the reins to Ryder. With one arm around the boy, he explained how to hold the lines and how to give commands the horse would understand. After making wobbling tracks across the fresh snow for several hundred yards, Ryder began to get the hang of it. It gave Ben a chance to check on the passengers behind him.

A tiny muffled voice shouted, "Text message!" Kimi pulled her phone out of her pocket.

Sally leveled an exasperated stare at her. "You were supposed to leave your phone at the house."

"Ryder is having fun. Why can't I have fun, too?"

"Would you like to take a turn driving Dandy?" Ben asked.

Kimi arched one eyebrow. "That is not fun. Texting my friends is fun."

"Suit yourself, but you're not going to get much reception up in these hills."

"How far are we going?" Sally asked.

"The McIntyre family owns five hundred acres of forest above Carson Lake. It's about three miles as the crow flies. It will take an hour."

"An hour round trip? You've got to be kidding." Kimi looked ready to jump out and walk home.

"An hour there and an hour back," he clarified. "Plus, we have to stop in to see your great-grandmother. That will take at least another hour."

Kimi pointed off to the side. "There's a row of trees. They look great. Cut down one of them and save us two hours."

Ben caught a glimpse of Sally's smile and shared her amusement before he remembered the conversation they needed to have. He couldn't do anything to foster her mistaken impression that he wanted to be her boyfriend. "They have been planted to make a windbreak along the field. I don't think our neighbor would like it if we cut down one that belonged to him."

Ryder looked them over and shook his head. "I'll know the perfect tree when I see it, Kimi. I get to pick. Grandma said so."

"Fine. Just make it quick." She leaned back and snuggled under the blanket.

Sally said, "Relax, Kimi. Enjoy the ride. Your grandmother is right. You'll never forget this experience." There was a wistful, husky quality in her voice that Ben found strangely appealing. Everything about her seemed different, somehow. He glanced back and found her staring at him. She gave him a sad little smile and looked away.

It bothered him to see her sad.

Ben took the reins and pushed Dandy to a faster pace. The sooner they finished this outing, the better.

The ride through the open country was as pretty as Sally could have wished for. The horse carried them along an old logging road that gradually climbed a long ridge of hills. It ran between stands of thick forest with open breaks that afforded breathtakingly beautiful views of the Amish farms spread out across the wide, snow-covered valley below. She couldn't see her father's farm from here, but it was nice to be this close to home. If only Ben wasn't upset with her.

She stared at his broad back and admired the way he handled Ryder and the horse at the same time. He would make a good father someday.

A stab of sorrow shot through her chest. He would be a good father, but she wouldn't be the mother of his children. She forced herself to admire the scenery and not think about the man handling the reins.

A few smaller roads branched off the main track as the road climbed, but they all led deeper into the woods. None of them bore signs of recent travel. After nearly thirty minutes in the sleigh, a lone deer ran across the road in front of them.

"Do you hunt, Ben?" Ryder asked.

"I go hunting with my *daed* and my older brother Adrian every year."

"I didn't think the Amish touched guns," Kimi said in surprise.

Ben glanced back at her. "We do for hunting, but we can never raise a gun against a man."

"But you can shoot someone to protect yourself, can't you?" Ryder asked.

Ben shook his head. "No, never. We must pray for the wrongdoers. Our lives are in God's hands, not in our own."

"The Amish must submit meekly to those who would harm us," Sally said, failing to keep the bitterness out of her tone.

"That's messed up," Kimi said.

"Yes, it is," Sally agreed softly. She kept her eyes on Ben's back, but he didn't turn around. She wasn't meek and she didn't have to pretend that she was anymore.

It started to snow a short time later. The flakes were small and light and added to the beauty of the ride. Sally relaxed and started enjoying the quiet stillness of the snow-covered woods. The only sounds were the hiss of the sleigh runners gliding over the snow, the jingle of harness bells and Ryder's occasional questions. It was never this quiet in the city.

At last, Ben drew Dandy to a stop. "This is it."

Off to the side of the road stretched a wide-open, gently sloping hillside with hundreds of trees that were only a few years old. Sally realized why Mrs. McIntyre had sent them here. About thirty acres of forest had been clear-cut. The replanted trees, mostly white pine and balsam fir, were just the right size for the McIntyre's great room.

Kimi threw her lap robe on the floor of the sleigh and

got out first. She took Ryder by the hand and led him to the closest tree. "This one is perfect. Get your saw."

"No, it's crooked."

"Okay." She led him to another. "This one is straight."

"But it's got a hole in the branches. See?" He ran down the row, stopping every few trees and then running on.

"Don't go far, Ryder," Sally called after him. It wouldn't take much for the energetic boy to get confused in the maze of green.

"I won't."

"Tell me what you do if you get lost," she said.

"I stay put and you'll come get me."

"That's right."

"Or follow your tracks back here if you can't see us," Ben said as he got down from his seat. Ryder waved and kept going.

"I should go with them," Sally stood up.

"We need to talk, Sally."

She decided to ignore his comment. She didn't want to talk to him. She just wanted the day to be over. "I'm going to follow the children."

He stepped in front of her to block her way as she tried to rush past him. Her feet tangled in Kimi's lap robe. She tripped and fell headlong out of the sleigh and into Ben's arms. The impact sent him backwards into the snow with Sally on top of him. Stunned, they lay face-to-face, staring at one another.

Chapter Four

Surprised, Ben lay in the snow with Sally clasped to his chest. Her face was inches from his. There were snowflakes caught on the tips of her thick lashes. He stared into her wide, startled eyes. Bright cornflower blue, they had tiny streaks of silver in them. He'd never noticed that before. The freckles scattered across her nose were downright cute. Her lips were parted ever so slightly.

What would it be like to kiss her?

She closed her eyes and his scattered wits returned. What was he thinking? He was not about to kiss Sally Yoder. Ever. She was doing it again. Throwing herself at him. This time literally.

He rolled to the side, depositing her in a fresh drift of snow as he scrambled to his feet. "Stop this foolishness, Sally. I'm not going to date you even if you throw yourself at me all day. If you were the last woman on earth, I'd still think twice about marrying you."

Her wide eyes filled with tears. Her bottom lip quivered pitifully before she bit down on it. Remorse sucked the air from Ben's lungs. He'd gone too far. It wasn't his intention to be hurtful. Sometimes, she brought out the worst in him. He extended a hand to help her up. "I'm sorry."

She blinked furiously and batted his hand away. "I

wouldn't marry you, Ben Lapp, if you were the last man on earth and you begged me on bended knee. And I wouldn't have to think twice about it."

Jumping to her feet, she furiously brushed the snow from her clothes. "And I did *not* throw myself at you. I tripped."

"Well, excuse me for jumping to the wrong conclusion, but you've given me plenty of reason to expect such behavior."

Her chin came up as she faced him and blinked away her tears. She took a deep breath and shoved her hands in her coat pockets. "I admit that I may have behaved badly in the past, but I got over that teenage silliness ages ago. If you thought otherwise, that is your mistake."

She pushed past him and moved to stand beside the horse. Staring straight ahead, she said, "I did not want to come to the farm, but I couldn't talk Mrs. Higgins out of it. I *really* did not want to come on this outing today, but Mrs. McIntyre insisted. I'm not here because I'm dying to spend time with you, Ben. The truth is I'm dying to get back to the house. Go help Ryder find a tree so we can put an end to this painful situation."

He sighed. "I didn't say having you here was painful."

She turned around and glared at him. "Frankly, I don't care. It's becoming unbearable for me. Go make sure the *kinder* don't get lost."

He scowled. Now she was going to boss him around? "I thought watching the children was your job?"

"Fine. Stay here and watch the horse, stable boy." As she stomped away, he could tell she was still fuming by the way she kept her head up. Better to have her mad at him than to have her in tears. He couldn't bear it when a woman cried.

Her forceful steps sent her braid swaying again and drew his attention to the curve of her figure in her jeans.

She was an attractive woman, he had to admit that much. Maybe he hadn't noticed it before because he'd spent all his time trying to avoid her.

It wasn't until she vanished from sight behind a curtain of white that he realized how heavy the snow had gotten.

I'm not going to cry. Not over him.

Sally wiped the moisture from her eyes. She got it. He was not now, nor would he ever be, interested in her. Good, because she was done being interested in him.

Although it had felt amazing to be held by him, if only for a moment.

His words hurt, but she forgave him. She'd made a nuisance of herself in the past. She could hardly blame him for assuming she was up to her old tricks. This was exactly like something she would have done last year. Before she realized how much she cared for him. Before she realized her behavior might be hurting him.

Was he seeing someone now that she was out of his life? He hadn't mentioned that.

No, he just said he wouldn't marry her if she were the last woman on earth. Well, that was good because she wasn't staying Amish. She was a free woman who would control her own fate. She didn't need a husband.

She saw the children just ahead of her. She sniffed once more and composed herself. If she concentrated on her job, she wouldn't have time to think about Ben. She was being paid to take care of the children. She called out, "Have you found the tree you want, Ryder?"

"Maybe. What do you think of this one?"

She came to stand beside him and give the fir due consideration. "It's nice, but since I have never had a Christmas tree before, it would be better to ask your sister what she thinks."

"It's fine." Kimi said with her shoulders hunched against the cold.

"You think they're all fine." He walked around the tree looking it over carefully.

Kimi held out her phone and snapped a picture. "If it will make you feel better, I'll ask my friends what they think. I'm posting this to my social media sites."

A few moments later, she held the phone out so he could read the text. "Jen says it's the prettiest tree she has ever seen. And you know she has great taste. Her mother is an interior designer."

Sally wasn't quite sure what an interior designer was, but it seemed to satisfy Ryder. "Okay, this one it is."

"Goot," Ben said, coming up behind Sally. She took a step to the side, crossed her arms and stared at her feet. She was afraid of what he might see in her eyes. He ignored her and handed Ryder a small saw. "Trim away the lowest branches while I get the chain saw."

Ryder started working with enthusiasm, but he had only one limb severed by the time Ben returned. Motioning for Ryder to stand back, Ben gave a quick pull of the starter rope. The chain saw roared to life and the stillness of the snow-covered woods was replaced by the whine of the blade slicing through the wood. The smell of fresh-cut pine scented the air, along with gasoline fumes.

Sally felt a moment of sadness for the small tree as it toppled. "It seems sad to cut down a perfectly good tree."

"Why?" Ryder asked.

"Because birds will never nest in its branches. It will never tower above the landscape. It won't supply fuel to heat a family's home or be used as lumber to build something useful."

Sally noticed Ben was staring at her with an odd expression and she fell silent. A blush heated her cheeks. Would it be this way forever when she was around him? Would she always be so intensely aware of him? If so, it was a good thing she lived in the city now.

"The tree is being useful," Ryder declared. "It will remind us that it's Christmas and there will be lots of presents under it." He looked up at Ben. "Where do the Amish put their presents if they don't have a tree?"

"My parents put a present for each *kinder* on their plate at the kitchen table on Christmas morning."

Ryder's eyes widened in shock. "Only one present?"

Ben smiled at him. "Sometimes two. Nuts and candy, too. For us, Christmas isn't about getting gifts and such fancy stuff. It's about remembering our Savior's birth. He is God's greatest gift to us."

"Sally says the same thing," Kimi said.

"Does she?" Ben asked quietly.

Sally glanced his way and found him watching her with a soft look in his eyes that made her stomach do flip-flops. How was she going to get over him when he looked at her like that? "Just because I chose to live in the city doesn't mean I have forgotten the important things in life."

"I'm glad."

"Can we go now?" Kimi shifted from one foot to the other.

For once, Sally concurred with the girl's impatient attitude. The sooner they got back to the farm the better. Hopefully, today would be the last day she would have to spend in Ben's company.

"*Ja,* we should get going," Ben said as he took hold of the tree trunk.

"Finally." Kimi rushed toward the sleigh.

Sally should have followed her, but she found herself asking, "Do you need help, Ben?"

"*Nee.* Ryder and I can manage, can't we?"

"We sure can." The boy's chest puffed out and he grabbed the back end of the tree.

Sally followed the pair, noticing the way Ben shortened his long stride to allow Ryder to keep up with him. Kimi was already at the sleigh, brushing the accumulated snow off her spot in the backseat when they arrived. She plopped down and pulled the lap robe up to her chin. Sally cleaned off her spot and then the front seat while Ben and Ryder secured the tree.

"Danki," Ben said as she finished. Sally took her place in the backseat.

"What does *danki* mean?" Ryder asked as he climbed up beside Ben.

"It means *thank you* in Pennsylvania Dutch," Ben picked up the reins and turned the horse toward Granny Weaver's home.

"Danki." Ryder repeated the word. "How do you say horse?"

"Gual," Ben replied. "Or if you have a horse in harness, like Dandy is, you could say, *fuah. Mie gual* or *mie fuah.* My horse or my harnessed horse."

Ryder repeated the words and then asked, "How do you say grandmother?"

"Grossmammi."

"How do I say I'm having a wonderful time?"

"Are you?" Ben grinned at him.

"I sure am."

"Then wonderful is *wunderbarr.*"

Kimi kicked the back of the seat in front of her. "Enough with the questions, Ryder."

The boy leaned close to Ben. "How do you say my sister is a pain?"

Sally smothered a laugh at Kimi's outraged expression.

Ryder continued to quiz Ben about names for different things as they made their way down from the hills. He answered the boy patiently and even let him drive again. The snow continued to fall heavily. Sally noted with concern that the tracks they had made on the way up were almost completely filled in.

"I'm getting kinda cold," Ryder said from the front seat.

Ben pulled the horse to a stop. "Why don't you get in the back and get under the blanket with your sister. That way you'll be out of the wind."

Ryder jumped out and wedged himself into the backseat beside Sally. He pulled the blanket his way and uncovered his sister in the process.

"There's not enough room back here for him," Kimi complained. She yanked the lap robe back and held on to it as she glared at him.

"But I'm cold," he wailed.

His teeth were beginning to chatter, but Kimi was right. The sleigh was built to carry two people in front and two in back. It wouldn't hold three of them comfortably, even though Ryder was small. Sally got up and let him have her place. He scooted close to his sister. Sally tucked them both in. Kimi lifted the corner of the lap robe and covered his head. "Is that better?"

"Much. Thanks, sissy," came his muffled reply.

"Whatever," Kimi shot back, but her usual sarcasm was missing. Sally knew Kimi did care about her brother, though she tried to hide the fact. It was a rare moment when she let her affection show.

Once Sally had the children settled, that left her with only one place to sit. Beside Ben.

Would he blame her for this situation, too? Perhaps she should suggest that Kimi ride up front. She glanced at the children. She doubted Kimi would agree. Both children were cold and tired. And they weren't getting any warmer while she stood there staring at the empty space on the front seat.

Ben jerked his head toward the spot beside him. "Come on, get in. I won't bite."

She hesitated for a second, then quickly climbed in. "I'm more worried about being growled at."

"I won't growl, either. I'm sorry I barked at you earlier. Am I forgiven?"

"I reckon."

"Goot." He flicked the reins to get Dandy moving.

Sally tried to stay as far away from Ben as she could on the narrow seat, but the track was rough. The jolting ride caused her shoulder to bump against his frequently. Each time, she jerked away from him and muttered, "Sorry."

He finally put his foot on the dash to brace himself against the rough going. "Relax. I'm not growling."

"Yet." She pitched into him again.

"Yet," he admitted, but the touch of humor in his tone made her feel better. Ben really was a kind fellow. It took a lot for him to lose his temper. She looked back and saw the children huddled together under the heavy cover. At least they weren't complaining.

Sally glanced at Ben's profile as he concentrated on driving. His hat was pulled low on his brow and his scarf was up over his chin, but she knew how handsome he was beneath the layer of wool. Some girl would be blessed when he set his sights on her.

Some girl, but not her.

She struggled to ignore the twist of pain in her chest. Would she have stood a chance with him if she hadn't behaved so foolishly?

At the time, pretending to be smitten with him had seemed like an easy way to keep other young men from trying to court her and to keep her parents and friends unaware of her struggles with her faith and her self-worth. Behind her bright smiles, endless questions and outspoken ways hid a frightened and confused young woman.

It hadn't always been that way. One horrible night, two *Englisch* men had changed everything. Changed her.

Maybe if she had found the courage to confide in someone about what had happened, things would be different, but she had never told anyone.

"What?" Ben asked.

Jerked back to the present, Sally shook her head. "Nothing. Why?"

"You're staring at me."

"Sorry. I was lost in thought." She redirected her gaze to the horse. Dandy's breath rose in white frosty puffs as he trotted through the falling snow. He seemed eager to reach the warmth of the stable and the ration of oats that would undoubtedly be waiting for him. She should be as eager to see this day done, but suddenly she wasn't. Would this be the last time she got to sit beside Ben?

The wind picked up when they finally left the sheltering woods. The road was all but obscured in places where the drifts were creeping in from the fields. Ben drew the horse to a stop at an intersection of two rural roads. Sally sensed his indecision. She asked, "How much farther is it to Granny Weaver's place?"

"Half a mile, give or take."

"The weather is getting worse. Do you think we should go back to the farm instead of going on to see her?"

"I've been thinking about that, but she's expecting the children. I would hate to disappoint her. Besides, if we don't show up, she'll be worried. It's almost two miles to the McIntyre farm from here. All of us could use a warm-up before we head that way."

"I guess you're right."

"We won't stay long. Dandy can get us home through more snow than this. There's no need to worry."

It wasn't the snow that worried her; it was the wind. Even the big horse would have trouble lumbering through heavy snowdrifts if it got much worse. "All right. I trust your judgment."

Ben turned north and urged Dandy onward. The cold wind in her face made Sally pull her scarf higher on her cheeks and wish she could huddle close to Ben for warmth.

Wouldn't he hate that? It was better to freeze alone. She kept her eyes closed and her head down. She would turn into a block of ice before she asked Ben Lapp for a favor after today. Suddenly, Dandy stumbled and fell. The sleigh tipped forward as it jerked to a stop. Sally was thrown from her seat. She put her hands out, but knew they wouldn't protect her from the horse's huge thrashing hooves as he struggled to get up.

Her flight was cut short when she was jerked backward. It took her a second to realize Ben had grabbed her coat, saving her. She heard the children yelling in confusion but not in pain. Dandy recovered his footing and stood but took only two limping steps before he stopped.

Ben pulled Sally back onto the seat and held on to her. "That was too close. Are you okay?"

She clung tight to his arm. She took several gasping breaths before she managed to nod. "*Ja.* You?"

He studied her intently. "I'm fine. You have blood on your mouth."

She pressed a finger to her mouth. "I think I bit my lip."

"Let me see?" He put a hand beneath her chin and carefully examined her face. She could feel his fingers trembling, even through his gloves. She was trembling, too.

"What was that?" Ryder stuck his head out from beneath the blanket in the back.

Sally pulled away from Ben and turned to the children. "The horse fell. Are you kids okay?"

"Hello! I'm on the floor! Get off me, Ryder!" Kimi's muffled shout reassured Sally.

Ryder grinned. "She's okay. Her phone didn't break." Kimi surged to her feet with the device in her hand as proof and sat back with a huff.

Ben jumped out of the sleigh without looking at Sally. "I need to check on Dandy."

As he trudged forward, Sally realized she missed his strong arms around her. She needed comforting after her fright, but of course the horse was his main concern. He probably thought she would see his quick-thinking action as proof that he had feelings for her. She knew better.

If she wanted to be a strong, independent woman, she needed to start acting like one.

Ben lifted the horse's left front leg. When he put the animal's foot down, Dandy refused to put weight on it. He stood holding the leg off the ground with his head hanging low. Sally got down and joined Ben.

Snow swirled around them, leaving them in a white cocoon. They could have been alone in the world for all she could see of the countryside, but they weren't alone. They had two children in their care.

She stared at Ben's worried face. If Dandy's leg was broken, the patient animal would have to be destroyed. She didn't want the children to know it was a possibility. She kept her voice low. "How bad is it?

Chapter Five

Checking on Dandy gave Ben something to do as he willed his racing heart to slow and waited for his composure to return. He kept seeing Sally flying over the front of the sleigh and falling beneath the horse's flailing hooves. If he hadn't had his foot on the dash, if he'd lost his own balance, if he hadn't been quick enough...it could have happened.

God had been with him in that moment as surely as the snow was falling around him now. By His mercy alone, Sally had been spared a frightful fall...perhaps worse. Ben's heart thudded painfully at the thought. He glanced at her worried face. "Are you sure you're okay?"

Sally nodded. She pressed her hand to her chest and let out a deep sigh. "I thank God Ryder wasn't in the front seat."

"Amen to that. *Gott es goot.*"

"*Ja,* God is good. Ryder's first sleigh ride could have turned into a tragedy. I'm relieved to see he wasn't too scared by this. He's a very sensitive boy. Please tell me Dandy is going to be okay."

She was pale as the snow in the field around them, but she was thinking about the children and his horse and not her own close call. Sally Yoder was made of sterner stuff than Ben had suspected. Her time away had been good for her. Or maybe being in charge of the children had matured her.

Whatever the reason, she had changed for the better. He couldn't sugarcoat their situation, although he wanted to spare her further worry. They had two children to keep safe, as well as his employer's injured horse to look after.

He should have turned for the farm when he had the chance. Now it was too far for Dandy to travel. They were stranded in open country in a snowstorm. Mrs. McIntyre had put her faith in him and entrusted him with the children. He would do whatever it took to get them back to her safe and sound.

He patted the big horse's neck. "I hope it's only a sprain and nothing worse, but I can't be sure. He must have slipped on some ice under the snow."

"Can he pull the sleigh with us in it?" Sally asked.

Ben shook his head. "I'll not ask him to do that. I don't want to make his injury worse."

Sally peered down the deserted road in both directions. "Should I stay here with the children while you go get help, or do you think we should walk?"

"The *kinder* will be warmer walking. It's less than half a mile to the Weaver farm. There's nothing closer."

Sally glanced at her charges. "I don't think they've walked that far in their lives, unless it was at the mall."

"They can make it. We'll leave the sleigh here. I'll come back with one of Granny Weaver's horses to pick it up and then take us home. Trust me. That's our best option."

She licked her lower lip and winced. Pressing a hand to her mouth, she said, "I trusted your judgment minutes ago and look where that got us."

"That's hardly fair, Sally. The horse could have fallen anywhere."

Remorse filled her eyes. "I'm sorry, Ben. I shouldn't

berate you when you just saved me from a nasty fall. I'm still a little shaken. I'll explain to the children what we need to do while you unhitch Dandy." She walked back to the sleigh.

She wasn't fawning over him for saving her the way he expected. A few months ago, she would have gone on and on about how strong he was and how much she admired his quick thinking. Maybe she was telling the truth when she said she was over him. He wasn't quite sure why that idea bothered him.

He set about freeing Dandy and listened to Kimi's rant at Sally about incompetent drivers and stupid horses. When Ben heard her say that she was calling a cab, he almost laughed. Sally took a step back from the sleigh. "Please, do call a cab for us."

"I will. What's our address?" Kimi held her phone higher, turning it one way and then the other.

"Somewhere near the middle of nowhere," Ben said.

Kimi scowled at him. "That's not funny."

Sally held her arms wide, "Look around, Kimi. Do you see a street sign?"

"I can't get a signal anyway."

Sally stepped back to her side. "Then we should get going before we all freeze to death."

Kimi stuffed her phone in her pocket. "I'll wait here for someone to come get us. I'm not walking."

Sally slipped an arm around her shoulder. "You will walk. I'm not leaving you here. If I have to be miserable, you have to be miserable. Maybe the good Lord is just giving you what you asked for."

"I didn't think it would be this bad."

"Everything will be fine when we reach your great-grandmother's house. Ben will get another horse and take us back to your grandmother's farm."

Ryder said, "Come on, Kimi. I'm getting hungry."

"Oh, fine. Let's go."

Ryder grinned. He was up for a new adventure. He walked beside Ben through the knee-deep snow without complaint. Sally was not so blessed by her companion. Kimi's tirade ran the gamut of complaints about the cold to assurances that her father would see both Sally and Ben fired for getting them into this situation in the first place. After a quarter of a mile, the physical exertion finally got the better of her and she fell silent. Unfortunately, her brother began to lag, too. Ben briefly considered putting the boy on the horse, but knew the animal's uneven gait and broad back would make it difficult for the child to hang on.

"Ryder, would you like a piggyback ride?" Sally asked.

"I guess." He looked uncertain.

She crouched so that he could wrap his arms and legs around her. Ben said, "I can take him."

Sally stood upright and shifted the boy to a more comfortable position. "When I get tired, you can carry him."

He nodded and looked at Kimi. "Are you doing okay?"

"Not really. I'm cold. I'm tired. I can't feel my toes or my nose." She had her mittens pressed to her face.

"Stomp your feet to get the circulation going," he suggested.

She tried it briefly but stopped. "It's not helping."

Sally tried to encourage her. "We are almost there, Kimi. Think how amazed your friends will be when you tell them about this vacation."

"I doubt they'll believe me, but I know one thing. This is the last time I will ever ride in a one-horse open sleigh. I'll never even sing that stupid song again."

Ben tried to make it easier going for them. He trudged ahead of them so that he and the horse could tramp a path through the snow. He was amazed at how quickly the white stuff was piling up. If it hadn't been for the mailbox at the end of the lane, he might have missed the turn altogether.

He could barely see a dozen yards in front of them. Dandy limped gamely along, but Ben could tell he was struggling. If the big horse went down, Ben knew there was little he could do to save the animal.

He glanced back to make sure Sally and the children were keeping up. Sally's breath was coming in quick gasps. He stopped. "Are you ready for me to take him?"

She shook her head. "*Nee,* your bigger boots are breaking trail better than I could."

"Are you saying I have big feet?"

Her smile was halfhearted. "Keep walking."

If she was trying to impress him, she was doing a good job. Much better than in the past. Her flighty ways usually annoyed him, but she was serious and determined today.

"I see a house," Kimi shouted.

Ben turned to look down the lane. The outline of the white farmhouse and red barn could be seen just up ahead. Everyone surged forward with renewed energy.

Sally put Ryder down when they reached the porch. He stomped up the steps ahead of Sally and his sister. "We made it."

"We did. God was looking after us," Sally said.

Ben gazed at her tired face and said, "I'm going to put Dandy in the barn. I'll be in as soon as I can. You did well. The children are blessed to have you looking after them."

Speechless, Sally stared at Ben's back as he walked away. Had he just given her a compliment? That was something she never thought would cross his lips. Wouldn't it be wonderful to hear more such things from him?

She gave herself a quick mental shake. No, it wouldn't, because when he was nice it made it harder to ignore him. The sooner they got back to the McIntyre farm, the sooner she could shut herself away and never spend time with Ben again. She quickly hustled the children across the porch and through the front door.

Just to be out of the wind was a blessed relief. Sally's teeth were chattering as she helped the children out of their wet coats and mittens and led them to the kitchen stove. Nothing had ever felt better than the warmth radiating from the large black kitchen appliance.

"Thank goodness you are finally here."

Sally turned to see a diminutive Amish woman wrapped in a huge black shawl enter the room. Her cheery round face was wreathed with wrinkles and a welcoming smile. She had thin, wispy gray hair parted in the middle and drawn back beneath her black *kapp*. Her sharp dark eyes belied her age. At the moment, they sparkled with delight.

"Good day, Mrs. Weaver. My name is Sally Yoder. I have brought your great-grandchildren for a visit. Your daughter sends her love to you and her brothers and their families."

"It's such a pity that Velda is laid up. I would love to see her. I must get over there when the weather clears, although my old bones are telling me we're in for a stretch of cold. And it's a pity that my sons are gone today, too. They and their wives went into Hope Springs this morning. My daughters-in-law had some Christmas shopping to finish. I expected them back before now, but perhaps the weather has delayed them. They said they might stay over with their cousins in town so I wasn't to worry."

"The roads are starting to drift. It's possible they won't get back tonight," Sally said. The children paid little attention to their great-grandmother. They were huddled close to the stove and holding their hands over it to soak in the warmth.

Sally quickly added, "Don't touch the stove, children. Everything on a wood burning stove is very hot."

Mrs. Weaver nodded and smiled at her. "You must be

the *kinder heedah* Velda told me about? I'm so glad you have brought them here. Children, let me look at you. Now, you can't possibly be Ryder, for he is only a tiny baby."

Ryder stood straight and tall. "I'm not a baby. I'm eight years old."

"Where has the time gone? I see you have grown like a weed while I wasn't looking. And this pretty *maydel* is Kimi. I would know you anywhere for you look like your mother. Do you remember me?"

"Sort of. I think I met you at Grandpa McIntyre's funeral."

"*Ja,* that's right. My name is Constance, but everyone calls me Granny."

Kimi looked around and then shot Sally a sour look. "You told us there wasn't any electricity in Amish homes."

"There isn't."

"I see lights. I see a refrigerator."

Granny gave her an indulgent smile. "My lights and icebox run on propane, but we burn wood in the stoves."

Kimi frowned. "What's propane?"

"A form of gas. Like your father uses on his outdoor grill," Sally said.

Granny Weaver motioned to the children. "Come into the living room and sit down. The stove in there keeps it very warm."

Adjacent to the kitchen, the large living room contained four recliners in various dark colors, a blue sofa with a blue-and-white crocheted blanket over the arm, a glass-fronted china cupboard, a tall bookcase filled with books and a foot treadle–operated sewing machine in front of a large window. A small black cast-iron stove sat on a brick base near the back wall and radiated blessed warmth.

"What's a *kinder heedah*?" Ryder asked.

Mrs. Weaver frowned. "Let me think."

"A nanny," Sally answered.

"*Ja*, I could not remember the *Englisch* word. How was your trip in the sleigh? Did you enjoy it?"

"No!" Kimi said.

"I liked it," Ryder said. "Ben let me drive part of the way and I found a perfect Christmas tree."

"Then the horse tripped and we had to walk forever." Kimi dropped onto the sofa with a scowl.

"It was only half a mile," Ryder rolled his eyes.

Kimi shot him a derisive look. "You weren't walking. Sally was carrying you."

Granny's eyebrows rose over the top of her wire-rimmed glasses as she turned to Sally. "You carried the boy that far?"

Sally made light of her deed. "The snow was too deep for him and Ben had his hands full trying to keep our horse moving. The poor thing's foreleg was injured when he fell. Ben is putting him up in your barn. I hope that's okay. He may be here for a few days."

"Your Ben is free to use anything he needs. There is plenty of hay and oats. You *kinder* must be chilled to the bone. Let me get you something to eat and something hot to drink. How about some peppermint hot chocolate with marshmallow cream and poppy seed bread with butter?"

Ryder's eyes grew round. "Sounds *wunderbarr, gross-mammi*."

Mrs. Weaver chuckled. "Someone has been teaching you Pennsylvania Dutch. Was it Sally?"

"Ben taught him a couple of words so he's acting like hot stuff. You're not as smart as you think, Ryder."

"Kimi," Sally cautioned her with a stern look.

"What? He's. not." She pulled her phone out of her pocket and sat up. "Finally, a signal."

Sally said, "I'm going to see if Ben needs anything." He should have come in by now and she was worried.

Granny Weaver began to bustle about in the kitchen.

"You must tell me what you've been doing. Ryder, how do you like school?"

Sally collected Kimi's and Ryder's clothing and hung the coats over the backs of the kitchen chairs. She arranged them, along with the hats and mittens, around the stove so that they would dry before they left. She slipped her coat on again and went out. The snow was blowing sideways in the gusty wind.

She crossed the farmyard to the barn that was only a hundred feet from the house. The drifts were three feet high around the corners of the building and nearly covered a pair of low evergreens growing next to the walls. Pulling open the barn door, she stepped into the dark interior and waited for her eyes to adjust to the dim light. She saw a glow coming from one of the stalls toward the back and went toward it. She passed several stalls. Most were empty. One contained a black mare that looked as old as Granny Weaver. The next held a brown-and-white milk cow. Another held two brown goats that stood on their hind legs to get a better view of her. Overhead, she heard the clucking of chickens in the loft.

Inside the last stall, Ben was wrapping a length of cloth around Dandy's leg by the light of a battery operated lantern. The big horse turned his head toward her and whinnied.

"How is he?" she asked.

"It's too soon to tell. If it's an injury to the ligament, it could be serious. For now, all I can do is ice it several times a day and keep it wrapped for support."

Sally glanced around. "I only noticed one other horse."

Ben stood and patted Dandy's neck. "Mrs. Weaver doesn't live alone. Where is everyone?"

"Her family went into Hope Springs this morning and haven't returned."

"The black mare down there is too old and too small to

pull the sleigh through this snow. Unless there is another horse on the property, we may be stuck."

"We can't be stuck." She stared at him in shock.

"Believe me. I'm even less eager than you are to spend the night here."

"I doubt that. We have to get the children home. I'm responsible for them." She did not want to spend time with Ben in the close quarters of the old farmhouse. She kicked a corncob across the dirt floor.

"I'm responsible for them, too. I know I got us into this. I'll get us out. I'll walk back to the farm and bring a team out to fetch you and the children. It should only take a couple of hours."

She rubbed her hands up and down her arms as she listened to the sound of the rising wind. "You don't have to hike."

One side of his mouth lifted slightly. "I can't very well fly."

His teasing tone was almost her undoing. She looked around for another corncob to kick before she blurted out how much she adored his smile. "We can use Kimi's phone to call Mrs. McIntyre and tell her what's happened and then wait here until Trent arrives with another horse."

Ben thought it over and nodded. "That's smart thinking. I forgot about Kimi's phone."

"You've had a lot on your mind. The children are safe now. You take care of Dandy and I'll go make the call. Come inside and warm up when you're done here." She turned away.

"Sally," he called out.

She stopped but didn't look at him. "What?"

"I'm sorry if I misjudged your motives in coming along today. You've been a great help. I'm not sure how I would have managed without you."

"It's good of you to say so." She kept her voice flat.

She hated it when he was being nice to her. It was easier to keep her distance when he was angry.

"When I'm wrong, I admit it, Sally." He paused for a long moment and then said, "Maybe we can start over and be friends."

Sally closed her eyes. She could never settle for friendship when she wanted so much more from him. The only way to get over him was to make a clean break. She knew that, but the crumb of affection he offered made it painful to say what needed to be said. "*Nee,* Ben. I don't think that's possible."

She started to leave, but the outside door opened and Mrs. Weaver came into the barn. She held a flashlight and a wire basket. "Ben, it's nice to meet you. You can call me Granny. I need to feed my chickens and the goats."

"Granny, do you have another horse I can borrow?"

"*Nee,* my Nellie is the only one here. My sons have the other horses. Nellie is getting a bit long in the tooth, but I can't bear to part with her. She has pulled my cart for twenty years. How is your horse?"

Ben left the stall and stopped beside Sally. "Dandy will be better for some rest. It took a lot out of him to hobble so far in the snow."

"It took a lot out of all of you. I had Kimi call Velda for me. I explained to her that you would be staying with me. She was happy to know all of you are safe. She'll send someone to fetch you when the weather breaks."

Sally crossed her arms and glanced his way. He shoved his hands in the pockets of his coat. "I reckon we can spend one night here."

"Might be more than that," Mrs. Weaver said cheerfully. "Velda said the weatherman is predicting a mighty blizzard. Could last three or four days. I knew we were in for a bad spell. My old bones have been aching something fierce. I can't tell you how happy I am that God sent you and the children to stay with me. What a blessing it is with my family gone. It will be just like a frolic, like an early Christmas party. We'll have a fine time together." She chuckled and turned to climb the steep stairs leading to the loft.

Had Granny said three or four days? This couldn't be happening, Sally thought, feeling the edge of panic creeping over her. How could she spend that much time with Ben and keep her feelings hidden? She had to find a way. She rushed toward the barn door and out into the snow.

Chapter Six

Ben stared at the barn door banging open and shut in the wind. Sally hadn't bothered to latch it in her haste to get away from him.

She'd said she couldn't be friends with him. What did that mean?

He had spoken roughly to her earlier that day, but she said he was forgiven. So why turn his offer of friendship down flat? Was she angry at him about something else? What had he done? He had complained bitterly about her to Trent, but she couldn't possibly know that.

He rubbed the ache in the back of his neck. He didn't understand why Sally pursued him in the past, and he didn't understand why she refused his friendship now.

If there was one thing that Sally Yoder could do well, it was confuse him.

"I like that young woman."

Ben looked up to see Granny Weaver coming down from the loft. She held a basket of eggs hooked over her arm.

"Sally is nice enough."

When Granny had both feet on the ground, she turned to him with a smile. "I know her family. They are good people. I hope she finds her way back to them. I pray that is God's will for her."

"I do, too." Ben took a pitchfork and tossed some hay in with the horse and milk cow. "What other chores do you need done?"

"If you will see that all the animals have water, they won't need anything else out here until morning. I like to gather the eggs a few times a day so they don't freeze while the hens are off the nests. I don't mind telling you that I'm happy to give over the chores to you. My old bones don't like going out in the cold."

"I'll take over the care of the animals. It's the least I can do in exchange for Dandy's room and board. He's a big eater." Ben went around to all the stalls and checked on each animal's water supply. He had to break the ice open on the tub for the cow, but the others had only a skimming of ice around the edges. By morning, they would all need to be chopped open.

Granny came out of the goat's stall. "I hear the wind howling like a wolf. It makes me happy the Lord has seen fit to give me a sound house to cover me and a good stove to keep me warm."

Ben took the eggs from her and followed her to the house, making sure the elderly woman made it across the yard without falling. Inside, Ryder was seated at the kitchen table. He had a white mug clasped between his hands and a chocolate mustache on his upper lip. A second mug with inviting steam rising above the rim sat across from him. Ben looked around but didn't see Kimi or Sally.

Mrs. Weaver hung up her coat. "I will take those eggs now. I have a lot of cooking to do. Christmas is just around the corner. I have gift baskets to make for a few of my *Englisch* friends and for a couple of elderly widows in my church. And I have a cookie exchange to get ready for.

That cup of chocolate is for you. Get warmed up. I know you must be chilled."

He was. He crossed the kitchen to stand beside the stove and snagged the mug from the table on his way. After taking a sip, he let the warmth spread through his body and savored the rich sweet peppermint chocolate combination. "Ryder, where's your sister?" he asked.

"Pouting."

Granny Weaver looked surprised. "Pouting? Whatever for?"

"She's unhappy because we won't be back in time to watch her favorite TV show tonight. She's upstairs in one of the bedrooms."

"I reckon I will have to keep her busy so she doesn't get bored," Granny said with a wink for Ben.

Ryder licked his chocolate-covered lips. "What can I do?"

"I have a chore for you boys. I need a large bowl of pecans shelled. Can you do that?"

Looking perplexed, Ryder shifted his gaze to Ben. "Can we do that?"

"It's easy. I'll show you how it's done."

Grandma Weaver fisted her hands on her ample hips. "Do you mean to tell me that you have never cracked pecans?"

Ryder shook his head. Ben said, "The trick is not to eat them all."

"I'll be back in a minute." Granny took a large wooden bowl from the shelf, opened the door at the far end of the kitchen and went down into the cellar.

"Where's Sally?" Ben had already noticed her coat hanging by the door so he knew she had come in.

"She went upstairs to try to tease my sister into a better mood."

Ben thought of Kimi's stubborn, uncooperative actions earlier. "Does it work?"

"Sometimes. Sally is better at it than anyone."

"Maybe because they're birds of a feather."

Ryder tipped his head. "Huh?"

"Because they are a lot alike."

"Sally doesn't get into bad moods. She's almost always happy except when she gets a letter from home. Then she gets sad. She misses her home a lot."

Ben glanced toward the stairwell. "Maybe she will return there someday."

"I hope not. Sally's my friend and I would miss her."

So, Sally could be friends with this *Englisch* boy, but she wouldn't be friends with him. Ben was determined to find out why.

"I'm not going downstairs, and that's final." Kimi pulled the blue-and-white quilt over her head and leaned against the headboard. She would soon run out of air beneath the heavy fabric, so Sally folded her arms and waited.

The upstairs bedroom was chilly, even with the warm air rising from the kitchen below. Lacy frost coated the windowpanes, obscuring the view. Even if she could look out, Sally knew there wasn't much to see. Just a lot of blowing snow that was trapping her in the same house with Ben. Sitting upstairs in a cold bedroom had seemed like her only option to avoid Ben, but she realized she was being foolish.

Since God seemed determined to force them together, Sally had to ask herself why. What was His purpose in doing so?

Maybe it was time for her to confess her foolish past behavior and ask Ben's forgiveness. She had used him. In doing so, she had compromised her own integrity. She cringed at the idea of explaining why she had pretended to

be head over heels for him, but if she had that embarrass-
ing confession off her chest, perhaps it would be easier to
deal with her current feelings.

Easier, but not easy.

Ben confused her. He made her feel breathless and
frightened, yet wonderfully excited all at the same time.
She wanted to be wrapped up in his arms the way Kimi
was wrapped in Granny's quilt.

This wasn't what Sally imagined love would be like, so
maybe it wasn't truly love. Maybe it was the kind of wild
infatuation that would burn out in a few months, rather
than the steady, gentle love shared by her parents for thirty
years. Maybe if she allowed herself to know Ben better,
she would see that he wasn't the ideal fellow she imagined.

If she told him the truth about her charade, he certainly
wouldn't want to be friends with her.

Kimi flipped the quilt down. "It's too cold to be out
from under these quilts, but I can't breathe under them."

Sally tucked her chilled fingers under her armpits.
"Welcome to Amish living."

"Why can't the bedrooms be heated?"

"Our parents and grandparents lived like this. We value
the old ways."

"Would it kill anyone to have an electric blanket?"

Sally ignored Kimi's question when she heard the sound
of Ryder's and Ben's laughter below.

"Everyone is gathered downstairs. Ben and Ryder are
doing something together with Granny. It might be work,
but they are doing it together and having fun. Do you hear
Ryder laughing? You are missing out. How many times
will you miss out on what he does before he's grown? How
will he remember his sister? As someone who laughed
and worked beside him? Or as someone he only saw oc-
casionally? Amish children know and love their brothers
and sisters well. Oh, we fight and make up like all people

do, but we spend time together as a family. It's very important to us."

Kimi pulled the covers to her chin. "Spending time with Ryder won't fix what's wrong with our family."

"Maybe not, but I guarantee that it would make him happy. You might find spending time with Ryder makes you happy, too."

"I doubt it."

"I'm going downstairs. I want to see what is making your brother laugh."

Kimi's phone giggled and shouted, "Text message." She pulled it out from beneath the covers. "Fine. Leave me up here to freeze all by myself. At least my friends want to talk to me. You just want to spend time with Ben."

"You should turn your phone off and conserve your battery. We don't have any way to charge it and we might need it. We don't have any idea how long we will be here."

"Whatever." She began typing a new message.

Sally shook her head sadly and admitted defeat. Down in the kitchen, she saw Ryder and Ben were cracking nuts. A piece of shell flew out of Ryder's nutcracker and landed in Ben's hair. Ryder dissolved in a fit of giggles. Ben removed the offending piece and dropped it in the trash can beside the table.

"I wondered what was so funny down here." Sally crossed to the table.

Ryder sat up straight. "Where is Kimi?"

"Texting."

"She should do this. It's fun." He squeezed a pecan between the jaws of a handheld nutcracker. The face he made while he was trying to exert enough force to break the shell made her turn away to keep from laughing. Ben had no such trouble. He laughed outright, which reminded her how much she loved his laugh. And his smile. And his kind eyes. Everything about him.

He operated a lever-action nutcracker mounted to a short board. He was able to crack five nuts before Ryder managed to split his. Once it broke open, Ryder promptly picked away the shell and ate the meat.

Sally grinned at him. "Are these for snacking or did Granny want some for cooking?"

"Both," Granny said from her place at the stove. She was smiling as she stirred something in a large pot.

Ben pushed an extra handheld nutcracker across the table toward Sally. "Want to help?"

"Come on, Sally, it's fun." Ryder gave her a big smile.

"I reckon I can crack more than you can. I know I won't eat as many." She took a seat across from Ryder and tried not to look at Ben. He was watching her. She could feel his eyes on her. She wished she were dressed Amish. It didn't feel right to be wearing jeans at an Amish table. It didn't feel right to have her head uncovered.

She sat working in uncomfortable silence while Ryder and Ben kept up a constant flow of friendly chatter. After a few minutes, Ben addressed her. "Do you like living in the city, Sally?"

"It's okay."

"You must miss your home and your family," Granny said.

"Sure I do. You must miss yours, too, Ben. Do you get home often?" The McIntyre farm was twenty miles from Hope Springs.

"Fairly often. I get back for church services every other week."

"So you get to some of the singings?" Would he mention if he were seeing someone regularly? How could she ask without sounding nosy?

"What's a singing?" Kimi asked from the foot of the stairs.

Sally kept her surge of joy hidden. Maybe her words had made an impression on the girl after all.

Granny answered before Sally could. "It's when Amish young people get together for a good time. We call it a singing, because they sing songs, but there is always food and games."

"Kimi, can you crack this one? I can't get it." Ryder held out his pecan.

"I guess." She took it from him, broke the shell easily and handed it back.

"Thanks. Can I play games on your phone since you aren't using it?"

"No." Kimi sat beside Sally. "So what kind of games do Amish kids play?"

"Volleyball is a game that we like in the summer," Sally said.

Kimi gave her a sidelong glance. "You play volleyball?"

"Kimi wants to make the volleyball team at school, but she isn't good enough," Ryder said.

Sally shook her head. "It isn't because she isn't good enough. She's just younger than the other players on the team are. They're all eighth graders. When she's older, she'll make the team. She has skills."

Kimi's chin came up. "I do have skills."

Sally grinned. "Amish kids play baseball, all kinds of board games and lawn games."

"I like chess," Ryder said.

"Me, too," Ben said, looking surprised.

"He isn't very good," Sally winked at Ryder. "You should play him a game."

"What kind of songs do you sing, Ben?" Ryder asked, dropping his chin on his hands.

"All kinds of songs."

"Even rap?" Kimi asked with a sly grin.

Ben began to pound a rhythm on the table. "Do you

know my face/I teach horses to race/I hate to roam/but I'm a long way from home. Do you like it? I just made it up."

Sally giggled at the looks on both the kid's faces. "No, we don't sing rap songs. Ben has been listening to the radio too much."

Kimi frowned at him. "I thought you couldn't do that?"

He said, "From the time we reach our sixteenth birthday until the day we become baptized in our faith, we are free to do the same things non-Amish people do. It's called our *rumspringa*. It's a time when we get to decide if we want to remain Amish."

"Being Amish is not an easy life, but we live it to remain close to God and to each other," Granny said.

Ryder turned in his chair. "Did you have a *rumspringa*, Granny?"

"I did. But the temptations of the world were not so great in my time as they are now. Young people now have a much harder decision to make."

"Were you mad at Grandma McIntyre when she left the Amish?" Kimi asked.

"*Nee,* I was not mad. Her father and I were very sad. It was her choice, we accepted that, but we worried that we would not be as close to her children and grandchildren as we would be to our others. In that, we were right. I see my other grandchildren all the time, but I don't see you enough."

Ryder stared at the pecan shells on the table and stirred them around. "Mom and Dad are always too busy to bring us here."

"I know, but I miss you nonetheless. I miss your mother, too. I think she is ashamed of her relatives who live without electricity and drive buggies."

Ryder looked up with a kind expression. "We're not ashamed of you, *grossmammi*. Are we, Kimi?"

Kimi looked at Ben. "You never said what kind of songs you sing."

"Most of them are from our songbooks. German songs and church hymns," Sally said quickly to cover the awkward moment.

Ben said, "We do sing some English songs. 'Amazing Grace' is one of my favorites. This time of year we sing Christmas carols but not modern ones."

"Let's have a little song while we wait for our supper to finish cooking," Granny said.

"Do you have a favorite, Granny?" Sally asked.

The elderly woman sat down beside Kimi and laid a hand on her shoulder. Sally knew it was a sign that she forgave Kimi for being ashamed of her, too. "I reckon my favorite Christmas carol will always be *'Stille Nacht.'* Ben, you start us off. The German version first, and then the *Englisch* so the children can sing, too."

With Ben's hearty baritone voice leading the way, Sally was soon singing along with many of the Christmas songs she knew and loved. For the first time since meeting Ben again, she felt at ease in his company. This was something they had shared in the past. It was part of the fabric of her Amish life and she missed it.

After twenty minutes of songs, Granny said, "I reckon the stew is done."

Sally rose. "I'll set the table."

Before long, they were enjoying Granny's wonderful beef stew with hot, flaky biscuits and apple pie for dessert. Only Kimi picked at her food. It wasn't the fare she was used to. When the meal was done, Granny said, "Our singing has truly put me in the Christmas spirit. I have been remiss in not setting out my candles. Kimi, would you help me? Ben, can you bring in some greenery? There are some evergreens beside the barn. They donate branches each year to help celebrate our Lord's birth."

Kimi got up and headed for the stairs. "I should check my messages."

Sally's heart sank. She knew what was wrong with Kimi. The girl was afraid to admit she cared about others. She was trying to be as unconnected as her mother.

"I'll be happy to get some greenery." Ben rose from the table and went to put on his coat and boots. "I have to check on Dandy, anyway."

Ryder jumped down from his chair. "Can I come? I want to visit Dandy. He might be lonely out there by himself."

"Not right now."

Ryder accepted Ben's pronouncement with nothing more than a slight frown. "Okay." He headed for the stairs. "Kimi, can I play a game on your phone? Please? It's my turn now."

Sally began to clear the table. She heard Ben go out, but less than a minute later, the door opened and he came back in. She looked up in surprise. Snow was plastered on his clothing. "Did you forget something?"

"No, but I can't find the barn."

"Are you serious?" Sally and Granny grabbed their coats and stepped out onto the porch. The house offered some shelter from the fierce wind, but it was bitterly cold. There was nothing visible beyond the porch steps but a curtain of white. The snow was blowing sideways. It was so thick nothing could be seen beyond the end of the steps.

"I've never seen a whiteout like this before." Ben had to shout to be heard over the wind.

Granny wrapped her arms around her middle. "You were smart not to try to make it to the barn."

"Dandy needs the wrapping on his leg checked to make sure it's not too tight if it has started swelling."

Sally remembered something she had read. "We can string a rope between the house and the barn so you can find your way."

The elderly woman started back into the house. "I have several lengths of clothesline in the cellar we can use. I'll get them."

Sally met Ben's gaze. "I'm not sure my idea is the best."

"It's a pretty good one. Tie one end to the porch and the other end to me. I'll head to where the barn should be. When I find it, I'll tie the rope to the door handle and come back once I check on Dandy. If I can't reach the barn, I follow the line back to the house."

"Are you sure you have to do this?"

"Dandy's my responsibility."

Granny returned with the thin white plastic coated rope. Ben measured off how much he thought he would need and then added another ten feet. He secured the rope and tugged on the knot "This should do."

Sally grasped his arm. "Be careful. Don't make me come after you."

"If I'm not back in fifteen minutes, you might have to do just that."

"Don't think for a minute that I won't, Ben Lapp."

"There's the bossy Sally I used to know. I wondered what had happened to her." He stepped off the porch and was gone from sight before she could think of what to say.

Chapter Seven

Waiting for Ben to reappear turned into the longest fifteen minutes of Sally's life. She and Granny huddled together out of the wind while they watched and prayed for his safety. Sally strained her ears trying to hear a cry for help over the wind if he should need her.

Just when she thought she couldn't stand it any longer, his dark figure emerged from the blizzard at the foot of the steps. In that instant, she realized how deeply she loved him and how foolish she had been. Foolish to turn aside his offer of friendship.

Just because he didn't love her the way she loved him was no reason to spurn him. On the wall at the small community church where she took Ryder on Sundays was a poster. She knew the meaning of the words came from Corinthians. Love bears all things, believes all things, hopes all things and endures all things. Nowhere did it mention that love had to be returned. She hadn't truly understood that until now.

It was childish and shallow to think Ben's friendship was a burden to her or that she couldn't return that friendship. She would treasure the love she held for him, but she would never turn her back on him again. She stood aside so that he could come up on the porch. "I was about to come get you."

He pulled off his hat and shook the snow from it. "I ended up in the evergreens, but once I realized what they were, I was able to find my way to the barn door. The rope is secure, Dandy's doing well, and I have your greenery and two more eggs for you, Granny." He pulled them from his pocket and handed them to her.

Granny chuckled. *"Danki."*

They followed her inside and left their coats and boots near the door. Granny put the eggs in the refrigerator and carried the evergreen boughs to the windowsill in the living room, where she arranged them around a thick red candle. The spicy smell of cedar filled the room. After lighting the candle, Granny stepped back. "This light will remind all who see it that Christ is the Light of the world as we celebrate his birth in this holy season."

The warm glow of the flame reflected on the frosty glass of the window and made the panes sparkle with multicolored points of light. Sally felt a deep peace settle in her heart.

Granny sighed heavily. "I think I'll go to bed now. It's been a long day for me. I'll bring in some wood from the back porch if you can stoke the small stove, Sally."

Ben said, "I'll bring in the firewood and take care of the stoves. You head to bed."

"All right, I will. Bless you both for looking after the *kinder* and for helping an old woman. *Gott* will reward your kindness." She walked with shuffling steps across the living room and entered a bedroom beyond.

Ben started down the hall that led to the rear of the house. Sally followed him. If he was surprised by her company, he didn't show it. The back porch was a small enclosed space with a large wood rack along the wall. Cut logs were stacked nearly five feet high. A ringer washing machine and storage cabinets lined the other wall.

Sally grabbed several logs from the high stack. Ben held out his arms. She began loading him down with wood. It took until his arms were full before she found the courage to speak. "I would like to talk to you, Ben. I owe you an apology."

"For what?"

"For a remark I made earlier, among other things."

"When you said we couldn't be friends?"

She nodded. He said, "Can we talk inside where it's warm? My feet are freezing."

She glanced at his stocking feet and held open the door for him. "Oh! Of course."

After he deposited the logs in the wood box and added one to the stove, he sat in a recliner and leaned back with a weary sigh. "I hope we don't have any more excitement on this adventure, because I'm beat."

"I know what you mean. We can talk tomorrow." She welcomed the reprieve and started to walk past him.

He reached out and caught her hand. "*Nee,* I'm not too tired to talk."

His hand was work-roughened, warm and strong and he held her slender fingers perfectly. As if he had been fashioned for that single purpose.

She withdrew her hand and missed his touch intensely. She took a seat on the sofa and clasped her hands together. "I'm sorry I said we couldn't be friends. We can. I would like that, but you may not feel the same when I tell you that my pursuit of you for the last few years was just a ruse. I wasn't madly in love with you."

Not like she was now.

"Why were you dogging me if you weren't interested in me?" Ben asked in amazement.

It was hard and painful to explain, but he deserved to

know the truth. "I knew that you would never ask a girl like me to marry you."

"You aren't making sense, Sally."

"I made a fool of myself over you to discourage other boys from asking me out. It kept my parents and friends from pushing me to settle down and marry. I used you to avoid getting into any serious relationship."

"But why?"

"What does that matter? I didn't realize I was making your life miserable. I'm sorry for that."

"Sally, it does matter why. It matters to me. Not because you owe me an explanation, but because, odd as it sounds, I do care about you."

She stared at her hands. "You're just being kind."

"Isn't that what friends do?" he asked softly.

Her throat closed and she couldn't speak for the tears that threatened.

"I thought you meant you were leaving the Amish for good and that's why we couldn't be friends. Is that the case?"

She sniffed. "I truly don't know if I can come back."

"It isn't an easy decision, because it isn't an easy life."

Looking up, she asked, "Have you made your decision?"

"I always knew I would follow in the faith of my father."

"I wish I had your certainty. One way or the other."

"A man can easily straddle a fence, but he'll never get anywhere until he gets off. What's stopping you, Sally? I once thought of you as flighty and wild, but you are wonderful with the kids. You were a good friend to those close to you. Give me one reason why you should leave our faith?"

"I'm not meek."

He chuckled. "No, you aren't."

"Don't laugh at me."

"I'm sorry. That was wrong. I see meekness as accepting what God wills."

She rose and crossed to the window. Folding her arms tightly, she said, "I see it as a weakness that others can take advantage of."

"Who took advantage of you, Sally?"

She closed her eyes against the shame. She wasn't ready to speak of it. Turning around, she forced a smile to her stiff lips. "I meant our people in general. I didn't mean me in particular."

"You aren't a very good liar."

"I've fooled a lot of people for a long time."

He crossed the room to stand in front of her. He was so close she could feel his warmth. More than anything, she wanted to lean into his embrace. "You aren't fooling me anymore, Sally."

She gazed into his eyes, stunned by the compassion she saw there. "I've never told anyone."

"I'll never tell anyone, either."

Could she trust him? When she started to speak, all the words came out in a rush. "I was seventeen. I was driving home from a friend's house in my little open cart instead of the family buggy. It was a pretty Indian summer evening and I wasn't in a hurry. I was passing by the gas station outside Hope Springs when a man stepped out from behind a truck and held up a hand to stop me. I thought he needed help. The moment I slowed down, he grabbed my horse and a second man got out of the truck. They started laughing. The one holding my horse said I was prettier than the last few had been. The one from the truck came up and grabbed my wrist. He was so strong. I was scared." She pressed a hand to her lips and turned away from Ben.

She could see her reflection in the window and the way the light of the candle shone all around her. She could see

Ben, too. He didn't say anything. He didn't move. He simply waited.

"I knew what was going to happen when the one holding me leered and said he liked Amish girls the best because they didn't fight back. None of us saw the third man. He came from around the back of the station and told them to stop. The one holding me let go and they fought. I couldn't accept my fate or wait to see who won. I grabbed my buggy whip and I struck the one holding my horse over and over again until he let go. Then, I whipped my poor horse until we reached home."

"I'm so sorry. Something like that should never happen. God will punish them."

"But how many meek Amish girls have suffered a fate worse than mine at their hands? I get sick when I think about it."

"Yet God saved you."

"I saved me. The buggy whip saved me. I'm not sure God was even there."

"God is everywhere, Sally. He did not abandon you."

She sighed heavily as she faced the truth. "No, He did not fail me. My entire life I have been taught to believe that I must submit to evil and never, ever resort to violence in return. When God tested me, I failed Him."

Ben stepped closer. "God knows we are not perfect, Sally. We're human. Our Lord will test us many times in our lives, but He does not require that we live a perfect life. He only requires that we try to live as He wills. The only way to fail Him is by giving up."

Ben's kind words were a balm to her wounded spirit. She longed to throw herself into his arms and weep, but she couldn't. He had spoken to her as a friend. She had to behave as a friend in turn, no matter how much she longed to tell him that she loved him.

Kimi came into the living room. "Is there anything good to eat?"

Sally welcomed Kimi's interruption and stepped away from Ben with relief. "I'll fix you some church spread. I think you and Ryder will like it."

Kimi looked around the room. "Where is the brat?"

Sally scowled at her. "I have told you not to call your brother names."

"I thought Ryder was upstairs with you," Ben said.

"He was bugging me so I sent him out."

Ben took a step closer. "What do you mean you sent him out?"

Kimi walked toward the kitchen. "I told him to go check on Dandy."

Ben grabbed her by the shoulders and spun her around. "He went outside? How long ago?"

Kimi shook off his grip, but she must've recognized the fear on his face. "I don't know. A while ago. He came back, didn't he?"

Sally shouted his name. There was no answer. She raced to the front door. Ryder's coat and boots were gone. "I didn't hear him go out."

"We must have been on the back porch. I'll go get him." Ben began pulling on his boots.

Sally held out a scarf. "Be careful. Don't let go of the rope."

It was a useless caution. Ben knew how dangerous the whiteout conditions were. When he opened the door, a blast of wind almost jerked it from his hands. Sally stood beside him shivering in the icy draft. He shouted Ryder's name, but the boy wasn't on the porch. Did he know to keep hold of the rope? Ben went down the steps and disappeared into the chilling white.

"What's going on? Why are you yelling?" Granny came out of her bedroom dressed in her robe and slippers.

Sally closed the door against the storm. Kimi turned to her great-grandmother with wide, worried eyes. "I told Ryder to go check on the horse. I just wanted him to leave me alone. I didn't know it was so bad outside."

"Hush, child. He is in God's hands. The Lord is taking care of him." Granny caught Sally's eye. They both knew what this could mean. If Ryder hadn't held on to the rope, he could easily become lost in the blizzard. If that happened, the likelihood of his survival was next to none. Was it already too late?

Chapter Eight

The door opened and Ben stumbled in. Sally's heart dropped. He was alone.

"Ryder's not in the barn. I searched through the snow as far as I could reach without letting go of the rope between here and there. He could have been a foot away from me and I wouldn't have known it. You can't see your hand in front of your face out there."

Tears sprang to Kimi's eyes. "I just wanted him to stop bugging me. We have to find him. He's too little to be out in such bad weather." She started to pull down her coat.

Ben stopped her. "I can't let you go out there, Kimi."

Granny put her hands on Kimi's shoulders. "He's right. Getting yourself lost will not help your brother."

Kimi turned around and buried her face in her great-grandmother's robe. Mrs. Weaver's eyes pleaded with Ben to continue the search.

Sally said, "I'll go out."

"Not without me." He was shivering with cold but she knew he wouldn't stay inside.

"Do you have more of that rope, Granny?" Sally asked

"*Ja.* In the cellar."

"Ben, we can tie ourselves together and then tie one end of the line so it will slide along the main rope. That way we can search farther from the path without becoming lost ourselves."

"Good thinking. I'll get it. Put on more clothes. The wind cuts right through you." Ben raced toward the basement doorway.

Granny said, "My grandson has long underwear, pants and extra socks that will fit you. His room is at the top of the stairs on the right."

Sally charged up the steps two at a time. She pulled the extra clothing over her jeans as fast as she could. She knew every moment was critical. Downstairs, she met Ben at the door. He tied the rope around her waist and made a second loop around himself. "Hang on to me until I get this rope secured."

Sally checked the distance between them. It was only about three feet. "This isn't much line."

"We will make a first pass all the way to the barn if we don't find him. When we get there, we'll lengthen the rope and come back."

"How many times?"

"Until we run out of rope. After that…"

He didn't finish the sentence. He didn't have to. Sally understood. If Ryder had walked farther away than their rope could reach, he wouldn't be found in time.

Granny handed them each a flashlight.

"Are you ready?" Ben asked.

Sally nodded and followed him out the door. The wind almost pushed her off the steps. She had to grab hold of Ben to keep upright. When he had the rope looped over the guideline and secured, she leaned close to him so that he could hear her over the howling wind. "Ryder couldn't walk into this. He would turn his back to it."

"You're right. We'll search along the downwind side of the rope."

At the bottom of the steps, Sally let go of Ben's hand

and stepped as far away from him as the line would allow. She could barely make out his figure. Together they began struggling toward the barn, shuffling through the snow, searching with their feet. Sally was shivering within minutes. She had no idea how Ben could tolerate being out in this again so soon. Only the thought of what Ryder must be enduring kept her stumbling forward.

They reached the barn without finding the boy. Ben pulled her toward him and pushed her into the barn. To be out of the wind was a blessing. At least she could see and hear Ben now. He loosened the rope from around her waist and lengthened the distance. When he had it secured again, he brushed the snow off her face. "Are you ready? Do you need another minute?"

"Not with that precious child lost out there. I'm ready."

"You are a brave woman."

"*Nee,* I'm not. I'm frightened to death."

"Only a fool wouldn't be frightened. God gives us the strength to endure what we must. Let's go." He opened the barn door and they went back into the maelstrom.

Sally began shivering immediately. The brief time in the barn hadn't been enough to rewarm her. Again, they shuffled along the length of the rope, searching as they went. Sally called to Ryder, praying he could hear her, even though she knew it was hopeless. She searched with her hands and her feet, knowing she could miss him by inches. Her light was all but useless. When she came up against the porch railing, she almost broke down.

They had to find him. They had to.

Ben pulled her toward him. He pressed his mouth to her ear. "Go inside. I'll go back."

She shook her head. "I'm coming with you. We have a better chance of finding him together."

He nodded and retied the rope. "This is all the length we have."

"It will be enough." She had to believe that. She had faith. She would not meekly accept Ryder's loss. God made her stubborn for a reason.

Still shivering, they ventured away from the limited shelter of the porch and began their sweep. What if she was wrong? What if Ryder had walked into the wind? Were they searching in the wrong direction? Could he survive this long? Her feet and cheeks were growing numb already. The scarf around her face was frozen solid.

Suddenly, she caught a glimpse of something dark in the snow. She jerked on the rope to signal Ben. He stopped. She stretched out her arm, but couldn't reach whatever it was. Another few inches was all she needed. She slipped out of the rope and dropped to her knees knowing she had to keep her sense of direction. She crawled forward and touched something hard. It was Ryder's boot. She latched on to his leg. Ben came to the end of the rope. She held her hand toward him. He grabbed her and pulled. It took all her strength to bring Ryder with her. She couldn't tell if he was alive. He wasn't moving. Ben pulled them to his side and lifted the boy in his arms. Together, they struggled back to the house. On the porch, Sally threw open the door and stood back to let Ben inside.

He staggered in with Ryder in his arms, stumbled and fell to his knees. Shivers racked his body. Sally was chilled to the bone and Ben had been out twice as long as she had. Ryder had been out much longer.

Kimi stood plastered against the wall, her face white with shock. "Is he dead?"

"He's breathing," Ben managed to say through his chattering teeth.

Granny rushed in as Ben laid the boy on the floor. "Get his clothes off. I have blankets warming in the oven. I'll get them."

Sally pulled off her hat and scarf and tossed them to the

floor, along with her coat. She used her teeth to pull off her frozen mittens. Her fingers were almost useless as she tried to unzip Ryder's coat. "Kimi, help me."

Kimi pushed away from the wall and dropped to her knees beside her brother. "I'm so sorry. I didn't mean for this to happen." She managed to pull his coat off. "What do we do now?"

Sally looked at Ben. He said, "I'm not sure. Warm him as fast as we can."

Sally grabbed Kimi's arm. "Get your phone. We can call 911. They'll tell us what to do."

Kimi shook her head. "It's dead. I know you told me not to use it, but I wanted to talk to my friends today. The battery died while I was trying to call Mom. She didn't answer. I was leaving a message for her and Dad to tell them what happened to Ryder when my phone cut off. I'm sorry."

Sally wanted to shake the child, but it wouldn't do any good. She could see that Kimi was upset enough. "It's okay, Kimi. Be strong for your brother."

Granny came back with the blankets. She gave one to Ben and one to Sally. "Wrap yourselves up. Dr. White said, 'Warm them little by little and start in the middle. Warm them too fast and the good won't last.' My grandson Marvin fell through the ice at a skating party. By God's grace, he was rescued and Dr. White was fetched to take care of him. God bless that good man. Get all Ryder's wet clothes off. Leave his underclothes on if they're dry. Wrap this blanket around his body, but don't cover his hands and feet with it just yet. Keep an eye on his breathing."

Kimi quickly did as she was instructed. Granny spread a quilt over Ryder. His face was deathly pale and his lips were an awful shade of blue. Sally helped Ben out of his coat. He was shivering violently. She wrapped one of the blankets around his shoulders. He closed his eyes in bliss. She squeezed his arm, offering him comfort and something more. His hand came out from beneath the blankets and captured hers, holding it tight. He opened his eyes and gazed up at her. *"Danki."*

It was more than thanks for the warm blanket. It was his thanks for her help, but it was something else, too. There was intense emotion in his eyes. Afraid of reading too much into what she saw, she pulled her hand away. She wrapped herself in the blanket Granny had given her. To be warm was the most wonderful sensation she had ever known. Her hands started stinging as the circulation returned to her icy fingers.

Although he was still shivering, Ben managed to stand. "We should get him into bed."

Granny said, "It is warmer in the kitchen. I have a cot that I use when I have more company than beds. I'll get it and put it near the stove. Rest a few minutes longer, Ben."

He nodded and huddled deeper in the blanket as she left the room. Kimi had Ryder's head in her lap as she knelt beside him. She looked up at Ben. "I didn't want this to happen. You believe me, don't you? I love him. I know I say mean things to him, but I'm never gonna say anything mean to him again. He's going to be all right, isn't he?"

"We are doing everything we can. It is up to God," Ben said.

"If I pray, God will listen, isn't that right? Sally, you said God always listens to our prayers."

Sally knelt beside Kimi and put her arm around her shoulders. "He does. God always hears our prayers. He gave Ryder back to us tonight. We must have faith in His goodness. He will not abandon us."

A tear slipped down Kimi's cheek as she gazed at her brother and brushed his hair back with her hand. "It's almost Christmas. God has to be listening."

* * *

Ben moved Ryder to the cot as soon as Granny had it set up in the kitchen near the stove. Following her instructions, Sally placed a warm blanket under him and wrapped warm towels around his body. Ryder's color began to improve and he started shivering. Color flowed back into his cheeks and his lips. What worried Sally was that the boy didn't rouse. Kimi couldn't be persuaded to leave him. She pulled a chair up beside his cot and sat talking to him and stroking his hair.

After the adults conferred in the living room, Granny decided to take the first shift with the boy, leaving the others to rest briefly. Ben agreed and went upstairs to lie down in one of the bedrooms. Sally was as reluctant to leave Ryder's bedside as Kimi was. Granny said, "You need to go get some rest."

"I don't think I can close my eyes."

Granny squeezed Sally's hand. "He is doing as well as can be expected. You get some sleep, and I'll wake you in two hours."

"I would give anything if this hadn't happened."

"Bad things will always happen, my child. We endure them and wonder why, but *Gott* has a plan, even if we can't understand it. Sometimes we think we know the reason, but more often than not, we must rely on faith and simply trust our Lord. One day, when we stand before Him, we will see all that He has wrought. Until then, we are but the threads of the quilt He stitches and binds. We can see no further than the threads around us. Who could know that what I learned when my grandson fell through the ice ten years ago would be needed now? *Gott* knew and He gave me the knowledge."

"Having faith is not easy for me," Sally admitted.

"Holding true faith in your heart is harder than being

Amish and that's difficult enough. Anyone who tells you differently is either lying to themselves or to you."

"Surely, it's not difficult for you, Granny?"

"Of course it is. I pray all the time that I may be worthy in the sight of God. I'm not as charitable as I should be. I resent that my *Englisch* granddaughter doesn't come to see me and keeps her children away. And I can't abide my neighbor, Ezekiel Knepp. His old cow is forever getting into my garden because he won't keep his fences in repair.

"Only God is perfect, Sally. The rest of us must struggle with our faults. We strive to overcome our shortcomings. Sometimes we fail. That is when we must accept that *Gott* loves us for who we are, faults and all. Our sins are forgiven. That knowledge inspires us to try harder to live a life pleasing to our Lord. Do you understand what I'm saying?"

"What if I don't think I can overcome my faults?"

Granny smiled. "With God's help, all things are possible. It may take a lifetime, but someday I'm going to like Ezekiel Knepp. Of course, I'll have to outlive that old cow of his. Go get some rest. Ryder will want to see your bright and smiling face when he opens his eyes."

Kimi ran into the room and grabbed Sally's hand. "He's awake. I think he wants you."

Ben threw back the quilt and shot out of bed when he realized that no one had come to wake him. He padded downstairs in his stocking feet and stopped at the entrance to the kitchen. The cot beside the stove was empty.

"We're in here, Ben," Sally called from the living room.

She was sitting in a recliner with Ryder wrapped in a quilt in her lap. She looked tired but happy. Ryder's color was pink and his lips were cherry red. His eyes were closed. Kimi was asleep on the sofa. Ben relaxed. Sleep was the best thing for both of them. He walked over to Sally and squatted beside her. "How is he?"

"He won't talk, but otherwise he seems okay. He whimpers if I'm out of his sight."

"That's not too surprising. It must've been a terrible fright for him."

Sally stroked the boy's hair. "For all of us. Four days ago, I was standing at the window looking out at the city and I said that this was going to be the worst Christmas ever. I was lonely and missing home. But I have to tell you, seeing Ryder's boot sticking out of the snow last night was the greatest Christmas gift I have ever received."

"I know what you mean. I'll put some coffee on and take care of the animals, then I'll hold him for a while so you can get some sleep."

"The storm has not let up. It's still howling out there. There's no way Mrs. McIntyre can send somebody to get us. You won't get home today."

"I can get to the barn and back. Some smart woman told me to put up a rope."

"Make sure you use it."

"Are you going to start worrying about me?"

Her eyes softened and then she looked down. "Isn't that what friends do?"

As he gazed at her pretty face and the faint blush coloring her cheeks, Ben realized being friends with Sally wasn't enough. He wanted more. Was there any chance for them? Knowing it wasn't the time or the place for that kind of discussion, he rose and went out to do the chores.

When he came back in, Granny was cooking breakfast while Sally was setting the table. He could smell the coffee and bacon and it made his stomach rumble. He glanced into the living room. Kimi was on the recliner holding Ryder, just as Sally had done, except that she had an open book in front of them and was reading him a story.

"It's remarkable," Sally said softly. He hadn't heard her approach.

"What's remarkable?"

"The way Kimi takes care of him. Last night opened her eyes in a way a hundred lectures from me would never have done."

"I may be cynical, but we'll have to see if it lasts once she gets her phone battery recharged."

"I have a feeling that it will. He still isn't talking, but he drank some water and took a few sips of hot chocolate."

"Sounds like he is on the mend." Ben smiled at her and she smiled back. His heart did a funny little flip.

After breakfast, Ben sat down with Ryder. The boy began to whimper when Sally went upstairs to lie down. Kimi came over to sit on the arm of the recliner and said, "She'll be back. Sally isn't leaving you."

Ryder quieted. Kimi asked, "Do you want me to read you another story?"

The boy shook his head.

"How about a game of chess?" Ben asked. "You said that you like to play."

Ryder considered the request and nodded. Ben left him propped up in the chair and brought a second chair over beside him. Then, he moved a table with an inlaid checkerboard on it between them. The chess pieces and checkers were inside a small drawer in the table.

Ben looked at Kimi. "I'll play him one game, you can play the next."

Kimi shrugged. "I never learned."

"Kimi, would you like to help me make some bread?" Granny called from the kitchen.

"Sure."

She went into the other room and stood beside Granny. The two were soon measuring flour, mixing dough and giggling. Glancing up from his game, Ben could see they were both enjoying themselves, although Granny's spotless kitchen was becoming something of a mess.

When Sally came down a few hours later, she went straight to Ben's side. Ryder was asleep again on his lap. She sat down in the chair Ben had vacated when the chess game was done. "How is he?"

"He still isn't talking. He points and grunts or whimpers if he wants something."

She chewed on her lower lip. "Why do you think that is?"

"I'm not sure, but his little mind is sharp. He almost beat me at chess."

She chuckled and the sound delighted him. "I've seen you play. It wouldn't take much to beat you."

"If that is a challenge, you're on. I know I'm good enough to take you."

"Careful, pride is a sin and it goes before a fall."

"Let's just say it will be a one-sided match."

Ben took Sally's hand. She didn't pull away and that gave him hope. "The boy is going to be okay."

"I pray that's true."

"God was looking after him. Especially when He sent you to be his nanny. You have been the answer to this young fellow's prayers, whether he knows it or not."

"I was looking for answers in my own life. I wasn't looking to be the answer to anyone else's prayers."

"And yet you are."

She slipped her hand out of his and looked into the kitchen. "What are Granny and Kimi up to?"

"They have been baking up a storm. Bread, cinnamon rolls, and now they are on to sugar cookies. I think we will all be decorating them this evening. Did you get some sleep?" She wasn't looking at him, she was still gazing into the kitchen.

"I did. This is what I have been missing about Christmas."

"Being snowed in?"

"*Nee,* I was missing the baking and the preparations and the anticipation of everyone coming for holiday visits."

"You should go join them. I reckon there's enough room in Granny's kitchen for one more cook."

She looked at him and shook her head. "I should hold Ryder and give you a break. Besides, I don't want to horn in on Granny's time with Kimi."

"Ryder and I are fine. Go. You know you want to. Granny will secretly welcome the help."

Sally grinned and left him. Even though his arm was growing numb from Ryder's weight, Ben didn't move. He had a perfect line of sight into the kitchen. Sally tied an apron around her waist, and then in a move that surprised him, she tied a white kerchief over her hair.

Her outfit wasn't particularly Amish, but he knew she was inching back toward her roots. And it gave him hope.

Chapter Nine

Although Ryder still wasn't speaking, he managed to eat a little bit of supper that evening. He developed a cough and a slight fever that put the worry back in Sally's eyes. He slept on the cot, with Kimi on the sofa beside him and Sally in the recliner.

By the next morning, he seemed better. Outside, the blizzard continued and Ben began to wonder if they would be rescued before Christmas.

He sat in the kitchen in the early afternoon pretending to read a book while he studied Sally. She was knitting at the table. She had borrowed some yarn and needles from Granny and was working on a pair of matching scarves. Her needles clicked softly as she worked. He had never seen her so still. So engrossed in something. Sally always seemed to be in motion. He liked that about her.

He liked a lot of things about her. Had he been ignoring the woman he should have been getting to know better? If she returned to the Amish, he wouldn't waste any time asking her out. Should he let her know that was his intention? Would it make a difference in her decision?

Kimi came out of the living room and sat beside Sally.

Sally stopped working and laid her needles down. "How is he?"

"He's sleeping."

"Why the long face? Your brother's doing okay."

"I want to make him something special for Christmas."

Sally smiled. "Kimi, that's a wonderful idea. I know he would treasure anything that you made."

"It's just that I don't know what he would like."

"There's plenty of yarn. Do you know how to knit?"

When Kimi shook her head, Sally said, "I will be happy to teach you."

"I want it to be something special from me."

Ben spoke up. "He likes to play chess. You could make him a chess set."

Kimi turned to look at him. "How could I do that?"

"You could carve them from wood, or you could use some of Granny's wooden bobbins with symbols of the pieces drawn on the tops.

Sally brightened. "Or we could make some out of bake-able clay. It would be easier than carving, and once they're baked, the pieces would be hard and durable."

Kimi's shoulders slumped. "We don't have any bake-able clay."

"We can make some. It's easy. We have everything we need in the kitchen. It takes two cups of flour and a cup of salt. You mix that in a big bowl and then you add a little cooking oil and just enough water to form soft dough. We can make them different colors by adding a drop or two of food coloring. Once you have the pieces shaped, I'll bake them."

"That's an awesome idea. Sally, you're the best."

The two of them got to work and were soon shaping pawns, horse's heads for knights and slender columns with crowns and hats for the kings, queens and bishops. One set they left white, and one set they made blue. Ben went in to check on Ryder and found he was still asleep.

"Sally, are you coming back to Cincinnati with us?" he heard Kimi ask.

Ben stayed in the living room. He wanted to hear Sally's answer.

"That was my plan. Why do you ask?"

"It's just that you seem happy here."

"I am happy here. It's like home to me."

"There's something nice about being here, isn't there?" Kimi asked. "It's so peaceful. I think this old house must be full of love. Did you know Granny has been teaching Ryder some prayers when she sits with him?"

"I didn't know that, but I'm not surprised."

"Do you think God left us here so that we could become a better family?"

"I can't speak for our Lord, but I think you might be right."

"I don't want Ryder to know this, but I think Mom and Dad are going to get a divorce."

"Why do you say that? They are on a fabulous vacation together."

"I heard Mom tell Dad that this was their last chance. If they can't work it out, it's over."

"That would be very sad for everyone."

"Granny says the Amish don't believe in divorce. Is that true?"

"It is. We must choose our husband or wife very carefully. We must pray about it and we must listen to what God desires us to do. Once we take the vows of matrimony, they can never be broken."

"Isn't it hard to find the right guy?"

"It can be very hard."

"So why don't you want to stay Amish, Sally?"

"I do want to remain Amish, but sometimes I feel that God has other plans for me. I must do as He wills, not as I want."

"I hope those plans include staying with us. Ryder needs you."

"I'm not so sure he does, when he has a wonderful older sister who loves him as you do, Kimi."

"If Mom and Dad split up, he's really going to need you, Sally. He's not like me. He's going to take it hard."

"Maybe your parents won't split up. Maybe they'll work things out in Paris."

"Maybe." Kimi didn't sound convinced.

Ben returned to the sofa and sat down with his book. He hadn't been thinking about how much the children needed Sally. He'd only been thinking about his own feelings. Ryder was as dear to him as any of his nieces and nephews. By urging Sally to remain Amish, he would be sending Ryder back into a family that didn't hold God and each other at the center of their lives. How could he do that to the child?

No, Sally had to make her decision without his interference.

Something awakened Sally. She sat up in bed listening to hear if Ryder was crying. She heard only silence. The wind had stopped. She got out of bed. Through the frosted glass of the window, she saw stars glittering outside. Relief was quickly followed by regret. Her time with Ben would soon be over.

She crept downstairs to check on Ryder and Kimi. Granny had moved the children into her room. Opening the door, Sally peeked in. Everyone was quiet. She pulled on her coat and went to the front door. When she opened it, she saw Ben standing on the front porch. She hesitated, but she could see that he was smiling. "Did I wake you?" he asked.

She pulled her coat tighter. It was still freezing cold. "I think it was the stillness that woke me. It's over. Praise be to God."

He looked out at the night sky. "Have you ever seen such beautiful stars?"

She moved close to him. They weren't touching, but she felt an intense connection with him she had never known before. She gazed up and marveled at the beauty before her.

The moon wasn't out, but the stars were as bright as she had ever seen them. The world was white below and sparkling with reflected starlight. The sky above was black with a million twinkling pinpoints of light, glittering as if in celebration that the storm had passed. There was something reverent about the hushed world spread before them. "It's so still."

He said, "The world in solemn stillness lay. This is what it must've been like on the night of our Savior's birth. A great hush of anticipation by the heavenly host as they waited for the moment."

With the words of her favorite Christmas hymn flowing through her heart and mind, softly, she began to sing. "It came upon a midnight clear, that glorious song of old."

Ben joined in with his beautiful baritone voice and their duet became a prayer of thanksgiving. As the last syllable died away, they gazed at each other and Sally began to hope that this wonderful man cared about her.

"I didn't expect to hear caroling at this time of night, but it is a wonderful way to welcome the spirit of Christmas." Granny Weaver came out to stand beside them. "Could we sing 'O, Holy Night'? It feels like a holy night, doesn't it?"

"It does," Ben agreed. He began to sing, and Sally and Granny joined in.

"What's going on?"

They all turned to see Kimi standing in the doorway. She had a quilt wrapped around herself and Ryder, who stood in front of her peeking out like an owl chick with his red hair pointing every which way.

Granny moved to drape her arm around Kimi's shoulder. "We are just giving thanks that the storm is done and that Christmas is almost here. Come join us. What Christmas song would you like to sing?"

Kimi looked skeptical. "Not the one about a one-horse open sleigh."

Ben and Sally looked at each other and smiled.

"'Silent Night,'" Ryder croaked.

Kimi dropped to her knees in front of him. "You spoke."

He nodded.

Kimi pulled him close in a big hug. "You can talk for as long as you like and I will never, ever tell you to be quiet and go away again."

"Yes, you will." He sounded like a little bullfrog.

Kimi pulled back to smile at him. "Okay, I might, but I won't mean it."

"Sing 'Silent Night,'" he said again.

"We'll sing, you rest your voice, froggy." Kimi wrapped the blanket around them both. She began to sing in a surprisingly sweet alto. Granny, Ben and Sally joined her. Although she didn't know the words to more than the first verse, Kimi joined in every chorus until they were done.

"All right, children, back inside. I'll make us something warm to drink and then I'm going to read you the Christmas story from my Bible so you will know what our hymns are all about." Granny made little shooing motions at them.

Sally was once again alone with Ben. The closeness she felt earlier began to fade. "How soon do you think we will be rescued?"

"I think we have a few more days yet. I find I'm not eager to leave," he said.

"Not eager to get away from me? That's a switch."

He stepped forward and put his hand beneath her chin to tip her face up. "*Nee,* Sally, I'm not eager to get away from you."

Sally held her breath as he leaned in and kissed her cheek. Her heart exploded with joy.

"It's too cold to be necking on the porch," Granny said from inside the door. "Leave it until tomorrow."

"Yes, ma'am," Ben said as he stepped back. His soft smile sent Sally's heart racing and she knew she wouldn't get a wink of sleep the rest of the night.

Ben was rewrapping Dandy's leg early the next morning when he heard a strange noise growing louder. He didn't realize what it was until he stepped outside of the barn. A red-and-white helicopter was flying low over the hills to the south. It dipped into the valley and came straight toward him. To his surprise, it stopped and hovered above the corral at the back of the barn. The blades blew up a blizzard of snow as it slowly settled to the ground. Was the chopper in trouble?

He glanced toward the house. Everyone was out on the porch to see what was going on. When he looked back at the helicopter, the door on the side slid open and a man in a red-and-white outfit got out. Ben waited where he was as the man approached.

"Is this the home of Constance Weaver?"

"Ja," he answered.

"Are Kimi and Ryder Higgins here?"

"They are up at the house with their great-grandmother. What's going on?"

"Ryder is here? He's safe?"

"Ja. He is fine."

The man grinned widely, gave a thumbs-up sign to the pilot, and then pressed a hand to his throat. "The boy is safe. I repeat. Ryder is safe. Over."

The pilot returned a thumbs-up sign. The man in front of Ben held out his hand. "I'm Officer Jake Cameron. I'm with the Ohio Search and Rescue. We were dispatched by the children's parents to find them. They were under the impression that Ryder had been lost in the storm. As you can imagine, they were frantic when they couldn't reach anyone to confirm that."

"Kimi's phone battery went dead. We had no way to charge it. Please, come up to the house. The children are both fine."

"We are under orders to take them to a medical facility for evaluation. Their parents have insisted on it." Officer Cameron followed Ben to the house.

Ryder stood wide-eyed on the front steps. "This is so awesomely cool. A helicopter just landed in our yard. No one at school is gonna believe this." His voice was still hoarse, but he was grinning from ear to ear.

Jake introduced himself to the group and grinned at Ryder. "I am sure happy to see you, young man. We were afraid you were lost in the blizzard."

"I was. I let go of the rope and then I couldn't find it again. Sally always told me that if I got lost I was to stay where I was and she would find me. I was really, really cold, but I stayed where I was and she found me." He smiled at Sally.

"Then we all owe her a debt of gratitude."

"This is my sister, Kimi, and this is my *Grossmammi* Weaver. That means grandmother. She's Amish. Do you speak Pennsylvania Dutch?"

"I'm afraid I don't." The officer straightened to address Granny. "The children's parents are on their way back from Europe. They had trouble getting a flight out, but they will be in Cincinnati tonight. They have asked the children be taken to a hospital there for evaluation. Although they look fine to me, I have to follow my orders. I hope you understand."

Kimi spoke up for the first time. "Mom and Dad are coming back already? They were going to stay in Paris for two weeks."

"When they heard your message, they immediately

started trying to get back. They are very concerned about you and your brother."

Kimi rolled her eyes "That's a switch."

Although the officer looked puzzled by her comment, he turned his attention to Ryder. "How would you like to ride in our helicopter?"

Ryder's excitement faded. He reached for Sally's hand. "I don't know."

"It's a little scary, but your sister will be with you and so will I and our pilot. It's very safe."

"What about Sally?" Ryder gazed at her with frightened eyes.

"I don't have any instructions to take Sally with us. Just you and your sister."

Ryder wrapped his arms around Sally. "I'm not going without her. Kimi, tell him we aren't going without Sally." Ben heard the panic setting in.

"I'm sorry, son."

"No. No. I won't go. You can't make me go!" He screamed and began sobbing wildly.

Jake glanced at Ben for help. "I can't authorize another person unless they are a patient in need of medical care. I can't reach the parents to get their okay for the added expense of transporting another passenger."

If Sally got on the helicopter, would Ben ever see her again or would she be lost to him in the outside world? He had grown to care about her deeply in these few days, but Ryder needed her desperately. She was the one anchor in the boy's life. She could help him become a man pleasing to God.

Ben's hopes to start a courtship with her crumpled beneath the onslaught of Ryder's tears. "Contact their grandmother, Velda McIntyre. She can make the decision and she will cover the cost."

"Great. What's her number?"

* * *

Sally comforted Ryder but she really needed someone to comfort her. She loved Ben. She loved him more than she had ever thought possible. She wanted to believe his kiss meant as much to him as it meant to her, but she couldn't be sure. Did she dare tell him of her love? If he gave her some sign that his affection was more than friendship, she might find the courage. For a woman who wanted to be independent and in charge of her own life, she was miserably inept at telling the one person who mattered most how she felt about him.

Officer Cameron went back to the helicopter and conferred with the pilot. She hoped she would be able to go with Ryder, but she desperately wanted a reason to return to Ben. Had their kiss last night meant anything to him? It meant everything to her. She gazed at him, but he avoided looking at her.

When Jake approached them again, he was all smiles. "Everything's been taken care of, Miss Yoder. You are to accompany the children and to stay with them until their parents arrive."

Ryder's sobs tapered off. He wiped his nose on the sleeve of his coat and sniffed. "Sally can come with me?"

"Sally can come with you," Jake replied. "You and your sister should go collect your things. We'll leave as soon as you're ready."

Kimi threw her arms around her great-grandmother. "Thank you for a wonderful time and for telling us the Christmas story. I want to come back and learn all about how to make bread and rolls with you."

"That may take a while."

Kimi looked up and Sally saw tears in her eyes. "I have three months off from school in the summer. Would that be enough time?"

Granny stroked Kimi's hair. "Three months would be exactly enough time."

"Can Ryder come, too?"

"Of course he can. You are welcome here whenever you want."

Sally took the children inside and they packed up their few belongings. Kimi gently wrapped the chess pieces she had made for her brother in the wool scarf her great-grandmother had given her. When she had the gift carefully tucked in the small box, she looked at Sally. "Mom and Dad are never going to bring us back here."

"You don't know that."

"I'm making an educated guess."

"You're a wise girl, Kimi. Someday, you will be old enough to do what you want and to visit whomever you want."

"Granny Weaver is pretty old. She might not be here then."

"If God wills it, your Granny will be here for a very long time. Her mother lived to be a hundred, and Granny is only eighty-one."

"You always look on the bright side, don't you, Sally?"

"If I do, it's because I know that when God made the heaven and the earth, he put the greater light to rule the day and the lesser light to rule the night. To me, that means he wanted us to see the bright side more than he wanted us to dwell in darkness."

"I have a lot to learn about God."

"You've made a good start. Just remember, he doesn't have a cell phone number."

Kimi grinned. "He might not, but my friends do."

Sally shook her head and followed Kimi downstairs where Ben and Ryder were waiting for them. As the children headed toward the helicopter with Jake, Sally hung back. She wanted to promise Ben that she would return to him. She wanted to speak of her love, but after behaving foolishly for so long, she knew she had to wait for him to speak of his feelings first. When he remained silent, she tried to prompt him. "It was quite an adventure, Ben. I will never forget it."

"Nor will I."

There was something odd in his voice. He wouldn't meet her gaze. She tossed caution to the wind. "I'm going to miss you, Ben."

He cleared his throat and said, "Ryder and Kimi will keep you busy. God knew what he was doing when he sent you to them. They need you, Sally. You have done them a world of good. Continue teaching them the important things in life."

She didn't want to hear that the children needed her. She wanted to hear that Ben needed her. She wanted to hear that he would wait for her. "They won't need a nanny much longer."

"Then you'll be free to decide on the life you want to live."

"And if that life is among the Amish?" Would he be waiting for her and rejoice at her decision?

"If that is where you believe you belong, I will be happy for you."

It was so much less than she wanted to hear. What was wrong? Had she misread his feelings, making his kindness into more because that was what she wanted?

"And if I wish to live *Englisch*?" She held her breath.

He straightened and smiled at her, but the smile didn't reach his eyes. "Then I will be pleased to say I have a friend who is *Englisch*."

He thought of her only as a friend. Then that was what she must be. She looked away before he could see the tears she couldn't hide. "Goodbye, Ben."

With her head down, she rushed toward the helicopter.

Chapter Ten

Two days after Sally and the children left, Ben was able to leave, too. An Amish neighbor with a team of draft horses pulling a snowplow opened the lane for Mrs. Weaver's sons in their buggies. After promising to look after Dandy until he was fit to travel, Mrs. Weaver's grandson gave Ben a lift to the McIntyre farm.

Trent was overjoyed to see Ben return. "Finally. I hope you had a nice vacation while I was working myself to death."

"You look well enough to me."

"I managed. Mrs. McIntyre hired some temporary help yesterday. She knew you wanted to go home for Christmas. I heard you almost lost the boy. I'm glad I wasn't in your shoes."

"I wish I hadn't been in my shoes." No, that wasn't true. He wouldn't trade those remarkable days with Sally and the children for anything.

After packing a few things, he had Trent drive him home. Everyone in his family was delighted to see him, but he couldn't call up the delight he knew he should feel in return.

He wasn't the kind of fellow who would dwell on his mistakes. When he messed up, he would admit it. He learned from his mistakes. What he learned was that life wasn't the same without Sally.

The day after he arrived home, he attended a Christmas Eve singing being held at the home of Eli Imhoff. It had seemed like a good way to get his mind off Sally, but it wasn't working. There were two dozen young men and women from Ben's church group present as well as a half-dozen visitors from a neighboring community.

He stood by the back wall with a glass of punch in his hand. He didn't feel like joining the game being played. A nearby table was laden with good things to eat, but he found he wasn't hungry, either. He eyed the group of girls across the way. There were some pretty girls and some plain ones, but none of them had ginger-red hair and amazing blue eyes with silver flecks in them.

"I can't believe you survived being snowed in with Sally Yoder."

Ben looked over his shoulder at the twins, Moses and Atlee Beachy. Moses said, "Will we hear the banns read in church this Sunday?"

Ben shook his head. "Sally is living *Englisch* now."

"That's a shame," Atlee said.

"A shame for us you mean." Moses took a sip of his punch. "Now that Ben is a free man, half the girls in here will be waiting for him to take them home in his buggy, and you and I will be riding home by ourselves."

Ben didn't put much stock in their banter. "The two of you like to exaggerate."

"Ha!" Moses turned his back to the room and leaned closer. "Don't look now, but Wanda Miller is coming over." He and his brother shared a chuckle as they moved away and left Ben as the lone target.

"The pastries look good." Wanda gave him a shy smile but kept her eyes down.

Humble, unassuming, easy on the eyes. There was a

lot about Wanda that was exactly the kind of girl he was looking for in a wife. Except for one glaring problem. She wasn't Sally Yoder.

Bold and outspoken, Sally had a caring heart that was every bit as important as the modesty he thought necessary in a woman.

Wanda added a doughnut to her plate. "I heard about your adventure. I'm so glad you were able to save that little boy."

"It was Sally Yoder and Granny Weaver who saved him."

"Is it true that Sally has chosen to be *Englisch?*" Wanda still didn't look at him.

He sighed heavily. "Sally is taking care of two children who desperately need her. It is the path God has chosen for her."

"Our ways are not for everyone," Wanda said. Was that a smile twitching at the corner of her mouth? He wished that she would look up.

"*Nee,* they are not."

She glanced at him then. "She had quite a thing for you. She really made a fool of herself over you. People say she lacked *demut.*"

"Sally struggles with meekness but she is humble before God." He didn't repeat Sally's story. That was something that would remain between the two of them. He treasured the fact that she'd trusted him enough to confide in him. He treasured a great many of his moments with Sally.

No, that wasn't true. He cherished every hour he'd spent with her because he was in love with her.

The thought took his breath away. He loved Sally.

Wanda spoke again, "I'm sure that none of us are surprised she left, but it still must be hard on her family. I wonder if she even gave them a thought."

He frowned. "Sally cherishes her family."

The entire time they had been with Grandma Weaver, Sally had been trying to instill that same kind of love of family in Kimi and Ryder. Without her, they might never have understood the importance of caring for one another and having faith in God.

If he had spoken of his love, would it have made a difference to her? His mind told him that he had made the right decision. His heart told him he had made a terrible mistake.

Wasn't he guilty of assuming that he knew what God had planned for her? For all of them? When the children didn't need a nanny anymore, Sally might well return home. He could wait. She needed to know that. They were both young. Marriage was nothing to rush into. Sally had said that herself.

She cared for him, but did she care enough to come back when he hadn't given her an indication about the way he felt?

He loved her. She deserved to know that. He tossed his empty cup into the trash can next to the pastry table. "It was nice talking to you, Wanda." He started toward the door.

"Where are you going?" she asked.

"I forgot to tell someone something important." He ignored the puzzled look on Wanda's face and rushed out the door. Tomorrow was Christmas Day. He would spend it with his family, but the day after that, he would travel to Cincinnati and see the woman he couldn't get out of his mind.

Christmas morning arrived quietly in Ben's home. There was a small package on his plate when he came down for breakfast. He unwrapped a fine pair of calfskin

gloves that were lined with fleece. He gave his mother a
new teapot to replace the one she had chipped a few weeks
before. He gave his father a book of woodworking plans.
They were both delighted with their gifts. After breakfast,
he went out to help his father with the chores. When they
came in, his mother was already starting preparations for
the feast they would enjoy with their extended family later
that day. Now was the time to tell them of his plans, before
more people arrived.

"*Daed, Mamm,* I'm going to Cincinnati after Christmas."

"To the city? Why?" His father began washing his
hands at the sink.

Ben hesitated. There was nothing certain between himself and Sally. "I need to speak with…someone."

His mother stared at him for a long moment. "What
could be so important that you have to go all the way to
Cincinnati? It will cost a tidy sum to hire a driver to take
you there."

His father turned around, drying his hands on a kitchen
towel. "Will Mrs. McIntyre let you off work?"

"I have vacation time coming to me. Trust me when I
say it's very important, even if I can't really explain right
now." After complaining about Sally's behavior for two
years, he didn't expect his parents to understand his sudden change of heart. Before he said anything about his
new relationship with Sally, he wanted to make sure of
her feelings.

His mother tipped her head to the side. "Very important?"

"It's vital to my future."

She struggled to hold in a smile and turned back to her
cake. "You don't have to go all the way to Cincinnati to
talk to her. I saw her mother in the store yesterday and she
told me Sally's coming home today."

Ben wasn't sure he'd heard correctly. "She's home? She's here in Hope Springs?"

"Why would Ben need to see Sally Yoder, *Mamm?*" Ben's father looked confused.

"Because he's in love with her," his mother said with a soft smile.

"He is? Since when?"

She walked over and took the towel from him. "Oh, for ages now, Papa."

"Why am I always the last one to know these things?"

"Because you are too busy running a business, saying your prayers, keeping your wife happy and your children fed." She planted a kiss on his cheek.

"It's good someone notices all I do," he replied gruffly.

"Of course we notice, dear. Now, get changed out of your work clothes. Our children and grandchildren will be here soon. And bring in those pies I put on the back porch to cool."

Ben's father winked at him. "She's a bossy thing, isn't she?"

"*Ja,* she is. I just never noticed before."

Daed frowned slightly. "Sally Yoder, huh? She always said she wanted to marry you. I thought that was pretty bold of her."

Mamm went back to the stove to stir something. "I told all my friends I intended to marry you, Henry," she said. "When I was just twelve. Sometimes, a girl knows these things."

Daed chuckled. "When I was about that age, I told my brothers I was gonna marry Esther Chupp. Happily, she married Bishop Zook instead. I'm not sure I could live with a woman who doesn't know how to laugh. Reckon it proves your mother is the smart one in the family."

"It's good someone notices," she replied with a sassy smile. "Ben, you had better get going if you're going to get to the Yoder place and back in time to eat with us. I'll put dinner back an hour."

"Danki." He kissed her cheek and raced out the door.

Sally smiled brightly at her sisters and her parents. She chatted happily with her aunts, uncles and cousins who had arrived for Christmas dinner. She was determined that no one would know how truly miserable she was. She reached for the ribbon of her *kapp* and her fingers found it. She was back in her Amish clothes and it felt right.

She didn't question her decision to return to her Amish community and family. This was where she belonged. She knew that now with the certainty that she would never question again. She was miserable because she knew that she would come face-to-face with Ben Lapp one of these days and she would have to pretend that she didn't love him. She wasn't sure how that was possible, but it was something she would have to do.

She prayed God would give her the strength she needed.

"Is that another buggy I hear?" her mother asked, glancing out the window. "I'm not expecting anyone else, but what a joy to have more company. See who it is, Sally, and make them welcome."

Her mother scurried away with a tray of vegetables. Sally pasted on her fake smile and opened the door. "Merry Christmas and wel…" Her voice trailed into nothing. Ben stood hat in hand on her front porch.

He was every bit as handsome as she remembered and her heart turned over with love. She pressed a hand to her chest to stop the wild thumping. It wasn't fair. She wasn't ready to see him so soon.

"Hello, Sally. Merry Christmas to you."

She wrapped her arms tightly across her chest. "What are you doing here?"

"I came to see you. Actually, I was leaving for Cincinnati tomorrow, but then I found out you were here. Is there somewhere we can talk, just the two of us?"

She stared at her feet. "I'm not sure I..."

He grabbed her hand and pulled her along behind him toward his buggy. "Ben Lapp, what do you think you're doing?"

"I need to talk to you, and you need to listen to me."

She glanced back at the house and saw several of her family members watching them. "All right, but I don't like to be manhandled."

He stopped and spun around to face her, shock written on his face. "Oh, Sally, I'm so sorry. I didn't mean to frighten you. Please forgive me."

"I'm not frightened of you, Ben. You didn't hurt me."

He took a step away from her and shoved his hands in his pockets. "Would you please take a ride with me in the buggy?"

Once Sally got in, he climbed in beside her. He took off his coat and wrapped it around her. "Are you warm enough?"

"I'm fine. What is so important that you have to drag me away from my family's Christmas dinner?"

He steered the buggy down the lane and out onto the highway. "How are Kimi and Ryder?"

"Fine. Happier than I've ever seen them. Spending three days not knowing if their son was dead or alive while they tried to get back home was an incredible wake-up call for Mr. and Mrs. Higgins. They decided they would all go to Paris together, and then they will come back and spend New Year's with Mrs. McIntyre and Granny Weaver. I think their family is on the mend."

"God moves in mysterious ways, His wonders to behold. So does this mean you are going back to them after the New Year?"

She looked out the window. "I resigned."

He turned the buggy onto a narrow lane that ran between towering trees. Their bare, arching branches interlaced overhead and cast intricate shadows on the snow-covered road. When they were out of sight of the highway, he stopped.

"But why? Ryder needs you."

"He needs his mother and father more."

"I'm sure you could have found another job in the city."

"I knew it wasn't where I want to be. It was where I needed to be for a little while, but it is not the life for me. I will be joining the church in the spring."

"I planned to talk to the Bishop about doing the same thing. I'm ready to settle down and start a family."

"I'm happy for you. That you found someone."

He placed a hand beneath her chin and lifted her face so that she had to look at him. "Are you happy for me? Because you don't sound happy."

Tears filled her eyes. Her throat closed and she couldn't speak.

"Do you want to know who has captured my heart?"

She shook her head.

"We shared so many confidences in our time together at Granny Weaver's that I feel I can tell you anything, Sally. The woman I've fallen in love with is a wonderful Amish maiden. She loves her family. She tries to live her life in a way that is pleasing to God. I'm not sure if she is a good cook, but I suspect that she is. What I don't know, what I'm afraid to ask is, does she love me?"

Tears slipped down Sally's cheeks. "She's a fool if she doesn't."

He let out a sigh of relief. "I know for certain that you are no fool, Sally Yoder. Do you love me? I pray that you do, because I don't think I can wait another minute to kiss you."

Sally looked at him in shock. "You love me?"

"I think I have for a very long time. I just didn't know it."

"Oh, Ben, I've loved you for so long. You have no idea." She threw herself into his arms and kissed him with all the gladness in her soul.

When the most wonderful kiss in the world ended, Sally snuggled against Ben's side, content to be near him. Knowing she had a lifetime of bliss to look forward to, if God willed it.

Ben kissed the top of her *kapp*. "You are a wonderful woman, Sally. I feel so blessed to know you. I'll spend my life giving thanks to God."

"A week and a half ago I thought I was facing the worst Christmas season. If Mr. and Mrs. Higgins didn't decide to go to Paris, if Dandy hadn't fallen, if the blizzard hadn't happened and Ryder hadn't been lost, I wouldn't be here in your arms."

Ben chuckled. "I reckon God knew it would take a lot to get us together."

She cupped his cheek, her heart soaring at the love she saw in his eyes. "It took a lot, but He has given me the most wonderful Christmas ever."

* * * * *

Dear Reader,

Once again, I find myself in Hope Springs amid the Amish during the Christmas season. Actually, I'm snowbound today at my home in Kansas, but my heart is with Sally and Ben on their adventures in Ohio. These two characters have been with me for a long time. I just never knew their story. That may sound strange to you, but sometimes my characters won't tell me what they need or what they want. Sally and Ben were both like that. It took a lot of prodding before I learned their story.

Christmas is a time to prepare. We prepare our homes with decorations and lights. We prepare loads of food to make sure our friends and family have good things to eat when they visit. We pick the perfect tree and lay presents around it in preparation for Christmas morning. While it seems that a lot of preparation goes into Christmas, sometimes we do not make the right preparations.

Joseph and Mary had very few preparations to make on that first Christmas. They didn't even have a bed. They had to put their newborn baby in a manger. Yet they knew that their child was the light of the world.

I hope that this Christmas you think about His wonderful gift to us and I hope that you will put a single candle in the window to tell the world that you know the true meaning of this holiday.

Merry Christmas!

Patricia Davids

Questions for Discussion

1. Sally had been aware for a long time that she didn't fit into her community. Has there been a time when you knew you didn't fit into a particular group? Did you make a change because of that? If so, was it a change for the better?

2. Sally presented a good example to the Higgins children, even though she was unaware of it. How can we be a better example to the children in our lives?

3. Sally tried to keep her feelings about Ben hidden. She was in love with someone who didn't love her back. Do you think it is best to tell a person about your feelings for them, or do you think it is better to remain silent?

4. The Amish do very little outwardly to celebrate the holiday season. How can we show our joy in the season without adding to our outward trappings?

5. Kimi and Ryder have a very typical sibling relationship. Ryder's misfortune causes them to reevaluate how they express what they feel. If you have siblings, do you believe your relationship with them can be improved? How do you think you should go about doing that?

6. Amish teenagers are not so different from English teenagers. In what ways do you think the Amish tradition of *rumspringa* benefits or harms the young people?

7. Many of us will attend beautiful services in our churches this year. I would find it difficult to celebrate without the physical presence of the church. What parts of the church service do you enjoy the most during the season?

"Robin," Ethan said, just before his face appeared in the church belfry's open trapdoor, "come on up. It's perfectly safe."

He reached down a gloved hand as she put a foot on the bottom rung of the wrought-iron ladder.

"How does this thing work?"

"It's very simple. There's a tall pole with a hook on one end. I used it to slide open the trap and then pull down the ladder. When I'm done, I'll use it to push the ladder back up and lift it over the locking mechanism, then slide the trap closed."

"I see."

"Oh, you haven't seen anything yet," he told her, grasping her hand and all but lifting her up the last few rungs to stand next to him on a narrow metal platform. In their bulky coats, they had to stand pressed shoulder to shoulder. "Take a look at this." He swung his arm wide, encompassing the town, the valley beyond and the snow-capped mountains surrounding it all.

"Wow."

"Exactly," he said. "There's a part of Psalms 98 that says, 'Let the rivers clap their hands, let the mountains sing together for joy...' Seeing the view like this, you can almost feel it, can't you? The rivers and mountains praising their Creator."

"I never thought of rivers and mountains praising God," she admitted.

"Scripture speaks many times of nature praising God and testifying to His wonders."

"I can see why," she said reverently.

"So can I," he told her, smiling down at her with those warm brown eyes.

Her breath caught in her throat. But surely she was reading too much into that look. That wasn't appreciation she saw in his gaze. That was just her loneliness seeking connection. Wasn't it? Though she had never felt this sudden, electrical link before, as if something vital and masculine in him reached out and touched something fundamental and feminine in her. She had to be mistaken.

He was a man of God, after all.

Even if she couldn't help thinking of him as just a man.

Will Robin and Ethan find love for Christmas,
or will her secrets stand in their way?
Find out in HER MONTANA CHRISTMAS
by Arlene James, available December 2014 wherever
Love Inspired® books and ebooks are sold.